I0779686

Echoes

By
Dr. Afshine Emrani

Copyright © 2025 **Dr. Afshine Emrani**

All rights reserved. No part of this publication may be reproduced, distributed, or transmitted in any form or by any means without the prior written permission of the author.

<u>DEDICATION</u>

If you've lost a child, a parent, or a loved one…If your heart aches with a sorrow too deep for words…If you find yourself wandering through the shadows, searching for light — this book is for you.

Grief has a way of folding time, of making the past feel closer than the present, of blurring the line between what was and what is. Pain can silence the soul, but it can also awaken it. In these pages, you will find a journey — not just of loss, but of love, resilience, and the quiet miracles that guide us home.

I wrote this book with the hope that it will meet you where you are, hold space for your sorrow, and remind you that even in the darkest night, the dawn is already on its way. May it be a balm for your wounds, a lantern in your darkness, and a whisper of hope when you need it most.

FOREWORD

The night I decided not to die, the stars looked like surgical lights through the fog—cold, distant, indifferent to human pain. I stood on the hospital roof counting them, as if they were the pills I'd thought about swallowing, the lives I'd failed to save, the reasons to step forward or back. The night wind performed its own kind of surgery, slicing through my white coat with precise incisions, each gust a whispered invitation: *Jump. End it. Be free.*

In medical school, they teach you to heal in precise measurements: 10 milligrams of hope, 50 ccs of comfort, a carefully calibrated dose of care. They teach you how to measure life in heartbeats, breaths, the steady beep of monitors marking time. But they don't teach you how to measure the weight of a life in your hands, or how to stitch yourself back together when you're the one falling apart.

Each day, we put on our white coats like armor, wear our stethoscopes like talismans, and pretend that knowledge makes us invincible and invulnerable. The hallways echo with the percussion of urgent footsteps, the symphony of life and death playing in endless loops. We speak in a language of numbers and abbreviations, as if reducing pain to statistics might make it easier to bear: *BP 120/80, HR 72, O2 sat 98%.*

But there are some vital signs we can't measure: the crushing pressure of expectations, the dropping levels of hope, the irregular rhythm of a soul in distress.

I didn't jump that night. Not because I was brave enough to live, but because I was too afraid my body would end up in our own emergency room, my colleagues forced to pronounce the time of death for someone they thought they knew. So I stood there on that rooftop, suspended between earth and sky, between being and nothingness, between the doctor I pretended to be and the fraud I felt inside.

Peter made a different choice.

Last night, my friend — my colleague, my mirror — chose darkness over dawn. The news found me beneath fluorescent lights that hummed like flatlined monitors. I stared at Peter's empty office chair, seeing ghosts: his steady hands that had held countless lives, his gentle eyes that had witnessed too much suffering, his quiet smile that had masked his own pain. I wanted to ask him, to plead with him, "Peter, why didn't you tell us?"

But I knew the answer. Because I've walked that razor's edge between healing and hurting, between saving others and losing yourself.

Peter joins a growing constellation of the lost. In ten years, I've watched four other doctors choose silence: One calculated his final dose with pharmaceutical precision. Another transformed his garage into an execution chamber while his children's laughter echoed from the yard. The third sought freedom in gravity's embrace. The fourth used his knowledge of anatomy to ensure the bullet would not fail.

They don't tell you in medical school that every life you save leaves a scar on your soul. That empathy is a double-edged scalpel, cutting both ways. That sometimes the harder you work to keep death at bay for others, the more seductive its siren song becomes.

I see it in my patients now, the ones who survive loss only to drown in its aftermath:

Sarah, clutching her son's tiny hand in my office, trying to explain why Daddy's love wasn't enough to make him stay. Her boy's question hangs in the air like wispy smoke: "If we were enough, would he still be here?"

Eric, sixteen and already ancient, his sister's suicide note folded into origami shapes under his bed. When his mother found them, each paper crane carried the same message: "I'm sorry I couldn't fly."

Michael, gray at the temples but still a child in his grief, weeping over his father's decades-old choice. "I've spent my whole life trying to be perfect," he confesses, "as if achievement could resurrect the dead."

In my darkest moments, I found strange comfort in conversations with ghosts — brilliant souls who lit the world but couldn't bear its glare. They spoke to me in languages of their own.

Vincent van Gogh spoke in colors — blues as deep as midnight despair, yellows as bright as false hope, reds as fiery as a blood moon — each brushstroke a cry for help painted in rays of blazing light. His hands, eternally stained with paint and purpose, sketched maps of escape routes he never took.

Marilyn Monroe spoke in the language of masks, of faces worn for others until your own disappears. Her smile, a carefully constructed curve, held all the secrets of being seen but never known.

Robin Williams' voice came as laughter wrapped around pain, like bandages around a wound that wouldn't heal. His jokes were flares sent up from the darkness, signals that someone else might see and understand.

These phantom dialogues taught me something vital: Depression is not just a disease — it's a skilled assassin. It wears the face of reason, speaks in the voice of logic, presents its poisons as cures. It tells you you're broken, a burden, that the world would be lighter without your weight in it.

But here's what I've learned in the years since that night on the roof:

Every time the emergency room doors burst open, every time a heart starts beating again under my hands, every time a patient leaves our care stronger than they arrived, I'm reminded that life persists. It finds ways to bloom in the harshest conditions, like the stubborn flowers that grow in the cracks of the hospital parking lot.

Last week, a young woman came to my office. Her wrists bore the geographical scars of previous attempts, but her eyes held something new. "I didn't want to die," she said. "I just wanted the pain to stop. But then I realized — if I could survive myself, I could survive anything."

This book emerges from that space between survival and surrender, between the impulse to end pain and the courage to endure it. If you're here, if you're holding these pages with hands that shake from the effort of holding on, know this:

You might feel invisible, but I see you. You might feel worthless, but you are irreplaceable. You might feel trapped, but there are doors you haven't yet found.

Hold on. Even when gravity pulls hardest. Even when darkness sings sweetest. Even when dawn seems an impossible distance away.

The sun is always rising somewhere. Its light will spill gold across the sky, painting hope in colors you've forgotten how to see. But you have to be here to witness it.

The world is better because you exist. This isn't optimism. This isn't platitude. This is diagnosis and prescription, written in the precise language of someone who has studied both death and life, and chosen the harder path of living.

I'm still here to prove it possible. I'm still here to help you find your way back to light. I'm still here. And I'm waiting to show you how to survive the night.

Table of Contents

DEDICATION i

FOREWORD ii

CHAPTER ONE *The Unheard* 1

CHAPTER TWO *The Echoes of Silence* 11

CHAPTER THREE *Voices From The Abyss* 22

CHAPTER FOUR *The Dead Speak* 41

CHAPTER FIVE *Lost in a Dream* 66

CHAPTER SIX *The Tears of a Clown* 81

CHAPTER SEVEN *The Restless Wandering Spirit* 101

CHAPTER EIGHT *Over the Edge, Into the Abyss* 125

CHAPTER NINE *The Dark Star, Flaming Bright* 142

CHAPTER TEN *The Voice of the Broken* 157

CHAPTER ELEVEN *When the Dead Speak Louder Than the Living* . 165

CHAPTER TWELVE *The Weight of What Remains* 178

CHAPTER THIRTEEN *The Weight of All These Years* 188

CHAPTER FOURTEEN *The Space Between Heartbeats* 198

CHAPTER FIFTEEN *What Light Remains* 208

CHAPTER SIXTEEN *Where Light Takes Root* 217

EPILOGUE 225

CHAPTER ONE

The Unheard

The scream of tires rings endless in Jason's memory. It will happen any second now, again. The moment replaying itself over and over. The yellow school bus pulls up across the street from his cedar-hedged suburban house in the morning fog. The air brakes hiss, the bus driver flashes his lights, signals Jason. "Judith, you're late, hurry!" Jason in his dusty-maroon terrycloth bathrobe calls out, his 7-year-old daughter finishing breakfast and rushing headlong through the kitchen, while his wife Sarah smiles and tunes the radio to classic rock, playing "Come As You Are." Then out the front door Judith flies, school books and lunch pail clutched to her chest, down the cement steps and across the misty lawn. Jason at the curb, chuckling at the little girl's messy hair and Big Bird sweatshirt, waving her to stop for a morning kiss on the cheek. Then off Judith races, smiling and laughing and waving back, excited to see her best friends Katie and Jasmine, eager to hear them fawn over her family trip to Chuck E. Cheese's the night before, and to reach the school bus in time through the fog.

One second later it happens. As Judith is leaving the curb and crossing the street, a wind blows straight past Jason. A car horn blasts, tires screech, and the Oldsmobile Cutlass belonging to his elderly neighbor Reuben rushes by, close enough to ruffle the flaps of Jason's terrycloth robe. Instantly Jason's face turns chalk white. Like a marble statue he stands, unable to move. He wants to raise his hands, wants to scream, wants to cry out to her "Run Judith! Run! Move!" and wants to claw at the air to get there in time. Instead he watches helplessly as the car with its horn blaring and its massive 382 engine churning careens wildly past him, plowing by the flashing red warning lights of the bus, shearing off its metal STOP FOR CHILDREN sign, crossing the white line and plunging relentlessly ahead with its high beams pulsating and motor bellowing. As it roars past Jason his daughter's laugh, high and innocent, is cut off by the scream of impact. Then silence.

Seconds later Jason hears the whine of police sirens, the yelling voices. They're screaming in his ears. And because it's too late, again — just as it will always be too late — Jason senses the impenetrable darkness coming for him. He feels the rushing icy fog envelop him, swallowing him. Clawing at the walls of fog he screams out "Let me alone! Give me peace! Please!" as the darkness crashes over him and carries him off, ripping him from this world into deafening madness. And as he plummets into an abyss Jason Marks is plunged again into an even deeper darkness.

\# \# \#

Jason woke with a start, trembling. His face was plastered with sweat, his hands clawing at his pillow. He jerked upright and gasped, orienting himself, waiting for the nightmare to let go. At the edge of his vision he saw the bedstand, then the clock. It was 3 A.M.

Stunned, Jason fell back and stared into the darkness. His daughter's nightmarish screams still flooded his ears. Releasing the pillow from his grasp, he pushed the dream away. Still his brain remained on fire with the vision — his beloved Judith being crushed by the Cutlass' massive engine, his neighbor Reuben slamming on the brakes after it was too late. The dream haunted him. Being yanked back to the reality of Judith's death was even worse. Reality slashed like a razor blade inside his pulsating skull. Even paving over the black skid marks on the street in front of his family home had failed to ease his torment. He felt trapped in a fiery pit of Hell and wanted freedom, escape from the dream, the heartbreak, the pain, the tormenting accusations of self-blame. *I don't want to see this anymore!* his soul cried out.

But there was no escape. With a sinking heart, Jason realized there never would be. Always the floodtides of grief would come crashing in on him. Life without Judith! How could he go on?

His heart fluttering, Jason rolled over. His wife Sarah was awake and watching him.

"Jason?" she asked, in a soothing voice. "Honey, you okay?"

"It's nothing," Jason managed. His voice shook. He took a deeper breath and sighed. "Go back to sleep."

Sarah wiped his sweating forehead with her fingers, gently dabbing away the wetness. She stroked her husband's shaking hand. "What's going on?" she sleepily asked.

Jason tried to speak. Perspiration dripped from his brow. The flutter in his chest began to thud and pound. He gasped for air and tried to turn away, but Sarah touched his face and drew him gently back.

"Take a breath, Jason. Relax. Inhale."

Jason took a breath, exhaled, met his wife's serene gaze. He stared at her, his eyes wide, his mind spinning. Shame and disgust burned through him. All he wanted in this moment was to hide. "Look at me!" he blurted out, his face red. *"Look at me!"* he yelled, his voice cracking with the words, as tears streamed from his swollen eye sockets. "It's been two years!

And still I keep blaming myself, and having nightmares about Judith, the accident, and — and — !"

Sarah slid her arms around him. "Oh, Jason," she whispered, searching his face, kissing his eyelids. They lay that way, Jason's thoughts trapped in a dark place no light could ever reach. He felt lost in a maze of self-hatred, while Sarah stroked his tangled hair, sobbing as she curled into a ball of her own grief.

Twenty minutes later, his pillow drenched with tears, Sarah sleeping peacefully, Jason sat up. He rubbed his face, moved his legs over to the side of the mattress, and crawled out of bed. Suddenly he felt a wild loneliness, and a desperate need to visit his daughter's room.

He sleepwalked down the hallway. He drifted past the bathroom, noticing the wall where he and Sarah had scratched in pencil, inch by inch and year by year, how tall Judith had grown. Reaching his daughter's doorway he swayed. He closed his eyes, then opened them again. As he did, the blackness in the room leaped out at him like an uneasy spirit.

Turn on the lights. You'll be able to see better, Jason scolded himself. But once he touched the switch he felt unable to move, controlled by a clawing need to remain in the dark.

From the doorway Jason stared in. He could just make out the room. Posters of Pokémon characters enshrined on the pink walls. Little-girl perfume-infused unicorn pillows on the rainbow-quilted bedspread. Sneakers neatly stacked under the bed where she'd last placed them. Jason smiled to himself. When Judith was a baby, he had crept here every midnight to watch her sleep. That year, Sarah brought Judith into their bed, covering it with extra blankets, certain their child would freeze to death. Jason chuckled at the memory. Jason loved Judith like crazy. Even her second-grade teacher Mr. Shapiro said she was going to grow to be a real beauty, a heartbreaker. Yet that was a lie, a fantasy; Judith would never grow. She would remain frozen in time in this room, and in a time and place Jason couldn't escape.

Two years dead now, Jason's brain sighed. Two years since a piece of his life had died. Still he blamed himself. Why hadn't he checked both ways before letting her cross the street? Why hadn't he walked Judith safely to the bus? It burned in him — the knowledge, the disgust, the shame that he hadn't protected her, saved her.

Stop it, his mind warned. *You can't keep fixating on this.* He could feel them now, the drizzle of tears surging. *I've got to get away from here,* he thought. *Away from this room, before my thudding heart explodes!*

But the longer Jason stood there, his daughter's belongings tugging at his heart, the more his legs turned to mud. Thoughts clouded his sleepless mind. He kept seeing Judith's casket, carried on the shoulders of her grandfathers, uncles and cousins before being placed in the black hearse. How he wished he could hear sweet Judith's voice again, just one more time! How he wished the dead could reach out and speak to him!

Yet it was insane to wish this. Death was everlasting. Nothing about life made sense. And trying to find reason in the chaos was madness.

Wiping his eyes, his breath coming faster and faster, Jason left his daughter's room, and stumbled back to bed.

Crawling under the covers, Jason shivered. There was a darkness enveloping him here too, threatening to swallow him, in the sacred sanctuary of his own bed. Only wishing he could see Judith again offered peace. Head throbbing, he lay back on his pillow, and pictured his daughter serenely floating and smiling above him. She hovered over Jason, up by the ceiling, her golden hair spilling down and filling his vision.

"Our little girl is looking down at us," Sarah once told him. "Watching over us from Heaven." It was this hope Jason latched onto. Yet the moment Jason blinked away the tears and opened his eyes, she was gone.

Sarah was sitting up in bed now. "Jason, what's wrong?" she asked, searching his face. "Talk to me." Seeing her loving eyes, Jason broke out in sobs and hugged her tighter against him.

Sarah touched his faced, caressed his arm. Sensing he was at the edge of a nervous breakdown, she traced her fingers down his tear-stained cheek. "Never mind," she said. "Just take it one step at a time, Love." Her voice was calm, her heart searching for something to erase the burden of his pain.

"But what can I do?" Jason asked, confused.

"Get back to your writing. You said yourself your writing has always filled the void, the empty spaces. What about the book on Vincent van Gogh you were writing? You said your agent was crazy about it."

Jason's bloodshot eyes searched hers. "Sure," he said, "of course, you're right." And she was right; Jason had been obsessed with van Gogh's work since early boyhood, paintings like *Sunflowers* and *Starry Night* a coping mechanism for Jason's own emotional struggles. After Judith's funeral, he'd turned to van Gogh's art and his tormented letters to his brother, Theo, as a path to understanding his own suffering and turmoil.

Jason pictured those paintings now. Slowly the overpowering aloneness inside him melted. Miraculously, the terror of facing life without his daughter evaporated; he seemed almost happy. And Sarah was smiling at him now. *God, Jason thought, she is so beautiful.* Sarah had always been his bedrock, his inner compass, always filled him with hope, even during his bleakest times.

"The nightmares will pass," Sarah said, resting a hand on Jason's arm. "Everything will be fine in the morning."

"Yes, fine," Jason repeated. "Everything will be fine. You're right."

Sarah continued to smile, and after a moment Jason smiled uncertainly back.

"Good night, Jason," she said, leaning forward to caress his cheekbone. "Sleep well, baby," she murmured, and turned back onto her side.

Jason nodded. He lay on his back and took a few deep breaths, a feeling of hope starting to sink in. Still he stared up at the ceiling, waiting for the vision of his floating daughter to return. Waiting. And waiting. No Judith came. Only emptiness and silence, mocking him. Crushing him. Finally his hope flared out, and Jason closed his eyes, seeking freedom from the agony and the blame, praying for forgiveness, praying for peace. But all he found in the darkness was more silence, and his prayers went unheard.

CHAPTER TWO

The Echoes of Silence

Silence has teeth in the darkest hours…□

In the dead of night Jason jolted awake, startled by the insistent beep of his laptop, the old dream draining from his brain. He blinked his eyes and sat up, rubbing his perspiring temples, blearily realizing where he was. For just a second he had been back at his comfortable home in the suburbs, safe in bed with his beautiful Sarah. Coming out of the dream the darkness still vibrated with his wife's voice, with the hush of her breathing, the warmth of her body against his.

Raising his head sluggishly Jason felt his stomach churn. He scanned the cramped apartment — a three-room second-story sad-looking room in a faceless downtown building, the plaster crumbling and peeling, the radiator hissing. He rubbed his bloodshot eyes, trying to rub away and erase the pain of the dream. "Holy shit," he mumbled, then swiveled the cheap computer, its cracked screen and its glaring light out of his line of vision.

Jesus, his brain grumbled, his head killing him. Just a year ago he and Sarah had still been a couple. They shared a life, a home, a family, a future. Yes, that future had been fractured by Judith's death — but still there was hope. To Jason it felt like decades ago. Pockets of grief hung below his eyes. He reached out clumsily for the open can of beer on his cluttered thrift-store desk, sucked the liquid down, then crushed the can in his fist, letting it spill to the floor beside the dozen other cans. Beside the pile of dirty clothes, the ratty mattress, the junk-shop chair and the torn couch he'd dragged out of the dumpster to fill this pathetic room. Beside the stuffed brown teddy bear at his feet that once belonged to his daughter, the one keepsake Jason possessed, a beloved and raggedy toy Judith nicknamed Harold.

Looking around his home, Jason felt dazed. Noticing the time — *3 A.M., Christ!* — he cracked open another beer, and dampened his tongue with the warm brew. The light from the computer screen was too harsh in his face, so he turned it again, casting a probing light on the darkened apartment.

It mirrored his state of his mind — cluttered, disorganized, suffocating. A mountain of unpaid bills. Stacks of unwashed dishes. Takeout containers emitting a rancid odor that mingled unpleasantly with the stale air of the apartment.

Jason shrugged. Just last week his landlord, cranky old Mr. McFitz who lived downstairs, had warned him the rent was overdue. Jason's failures haunted him. Sarah had left, after the collapse of their marriage. In the end, she couldn't take Jason's ever-changing moods, his rage, his sorrow, their shrieking, ugly fights. She had moved on emotionally, long before engaging the attorney and filing divorce papers. Selling their home came next, and had fueled Jason's descent into this low-rent apartment above a blood bank, this everyday hellhole of drinking and pill-popping, despair and depression. All he had were echoes of the life he'd destroyed.

I've lost everything, Jason shuddered, hanging his head. Now they were both gone — Sarah and Judith — gone forever. He started to feel woozy, too much booze on an empty stomach. Yet he couldn't stop his brain from punishing him. *Everything had been good, so good! And then Judith died, and our world shattered!*

Jason sat back, sweating. He slumped in his chair, palms clasped around his aching head. Putting the shattered pieces together is why Jason had purchased a cheap laptop, and chosen to start up the podcast. A last-ditch effort at redemption, he thought. Yet *Echoes*, the podcast, had become just another foolish pursuit, another failure. Its audience had never materialized, and the few regular listeners dwindled with each episode. The numbers were so low that they spiraled Jason into deeper self-doubt. *Three days, and only fifty downloads?* Just one more futile attempt to replace the voices he'd lost.

In the darkness his laptop beeped. The recording app blinked, waiting. Jason leaned closer to the microphone, letting out a weary sigh. The room mocked him with its emptiness. It had been days since he recorded anything, weeks since he'd felt the thrill of creating something that could change his life. He felt more like a walking corpse than a man these days.

Echoes had once been a labor of love, a beacon of hope, a shot at breaking free from the suffocating mediocrity that clung to him like a second skin. Now, the podcast was nothing more than a fraying lifeline.

Jason stared at the laptop screen, the title of his latest, unfinished episode glaring back at him: *The Voice That Never Speaks*. How ironic. How pathetic. Here he was, a podcaster with no audience, and nothing to say!

In disgust he ran a hand through his hair, greasy from too many hours without a shower. Staring at him from every corner were the heaps of unfinished projects: paintings and sketches he'd started, the children's book he'd begun writing in honor of Judith, the scrapbook of family photographs he planned to turn into a memoir on grief, and the journals, diaries and notes for his unfinished Vincent van Gogh book.

Flicking on the desk lamp, Jason flipped through a worn book of van Gogh's private letters. He traced the words with his shaky finger, reading aloud a passage he'd memorized from years of study: *"What am I in the eyes of most people? A nonentity, an eccentric, or an unpleasant person…"*

Slamming the book shut, Jason groaned. He stared at the ceiling, mind reeling with the emotional pain. "I get it, Vincent," he muttered. "I really get it."

Squinting into the desk light, Jason felt beaten. He clicked on his computer, deleting yet another half-written novel from his files. Moving the *Echoes* files to the trash bin, his hand hovered over the keyboard, doubt creeping in. "Why do I even bother?" he asked. "Everything I touch falls apart." The podcast had been his last shot. He'd poured everything into it — time, money, passion — and for what? A handful of listeners who barely kept him afloat, and a growing sense of despair that this was all he would ever be.

Jason glanced at the clock. It was late — too late to be making decisions, but too early to surrender to sleep. He knew he wouldn't find rest tonight, not with anxiety twisting in his gut like a knife. There had to be something, some way to save *Echoes* before it became just another failure.

Yet the early days of podcasting had been different. There had been joy, satisfaction, purpose. How eerily he now recalled recording the first *Echoes* episode — he was energized, his desktop clean, his laptop shiny, his mind uncluttered. *And I spoke with passion about my subject!* Addressing his audience, he talked about the power of stories, and how they can connect people. His podcast themes centered around existential questions like "Why do we fear silence?" and "What stories do we never tell?"

Even his introductions seemed sparked by unexpected wisdom. "Have you ever noticed how silence echoes? It's in the quiet moments where the loudest truths emerge. That's what we're here for on *Echoes* — to talk about the things we hide from ourselves, the voices we keep locked away. Every week, we'll explore stories that resonate with the parts of us we don't dare to confront."

Jason stared now into the punishing glow of his computer screen, feeling the tears come. How quickly he'd lost that sense of joy, of purpose! It became submerged in grief and shock, then in painkilling drugs and alcohol. Jason's head streamed with perspiration. My once-shining purpose gathering dust.

Just like poor Harold, Judith's stuffed teddy bear. A haunting reminder tossed into a corner.

Plucking up the threadbare rag-like animal, Jason pressed it tight to his face, breathing his dead daughter in. The tears came hard now, pouring down his face. *Our baby! Our little girl! Oh, Judith, why? Why us, God? Of all the wicked people on the face of this earth deserving of punishment, why choose us??*

Thrusting himself from the desk, stumbling out of his chair, Jason wandered to the bathroom, the cold tiles sending a shiver up his spine. He splashed his face with cold water, hoping the shock would revive him. When it didn't, he stared at his reflection in the mirror, barely recognizing the man who stared back at him. His eyes were hollow, blood-red, rolled up to bulging whites, devoid of the spark that had once driven him. His face was gaunt, unshaven, the result of too many nights spent staring at the ceiling, lost in a bombardment of negative thoughts.

In a panic Jason opened the medicine cabinet, fingers trembling as he fumbled for the bottle of pills that promised an escape. It was a thought he had entertained too many times. The idea of ending it all, of slipping away into the darkness where the pain couldn't reach him, was becoming more appealing with each passing day.

As he clutched the bottle Jason's mind drifted back to the past — to memories of Judith. Her innocent eyes, her tender smile, her sweet high voice. Once, he'd been a loving father. Wasn't he the good dad, catching his toddler daughter as she ran into his arms, Sarah watching proudly from the doorway as Jason spun their laughing child in circles? Later, tucking Judith into bed, he and Sarah settled on the couch, and Sarah leaned her head on Jason's shoulder. "You're thinking about your book again, aren't you?" she asked with a wink. Jason chuckled, wrapping his arms around her. "Yeah, but it can wait. I've got everything I need right here."

Jason plucked at the pill bottle with his fingernail. He shook his head and the memories vanished. This is what happiness looked like, felt like, back when life had meaning. Back when it had potential.

Weeping, Jason unscrewed the cap. The pink pills rattled into his palm like tiny harbingers of oblivion. *How easy it would be. How painless. How quick.* The thought lingered, seductive in its simplicity. No more torture, no more failure. Just silence. Peace.

Jason's heart pounded, the only sound in the crushing stillness. He could end it all. The self-rage, the despair. Right here, right now. No one would miss him. No one would care. He'd lost any reason to keep going, to keep living, to keep —

Suddenly from the other room, Jason's phone buzzed, breaking the silence.

For a moment, Jason's eyes remained on the pills. Beads of perspiration exploded across his brow. *Sweet Jesus*, he groaned, as the phone buzzed again. Feeling his hand tighten around the medication he stared at his reflection and then at the floor. When the phone buzzed a third time he stumbled to the desktop, snatched the phone up, and returned it to the bathroom.

He squinted at the screen. Three messages, all from an unknown number. Great. Who could be texting him at this ungodly hour? Jason hesitated, then clicked on the three texts.

Jason Marks.

I have good news for you.

Are you ready to hear what the dead have to say?

Jason's heart skipped. *What the dead have to say?* He read the messages again, feeling an eerie mix of curiosity and unease. He typed a quick reply before he could second-guess himself.

GET LOST CREEP.

His shaky finger hovered over the SEND button. For a moment he felt a twinge of panic. He turned the phone's screen away from him. What this person was saying made no sense. Hear the dead? Impossible! It must be some crazy lunatic fan of his podcasts, somebody playing a prank, mocking him. Hell, it wouldn't be the first time.

Deleting his first reply, Jason quickly typed three words:

WHO IS THIS?

The response was immediate.

Someone who can save your podcast.

Meet me at The Silver Spoon. 6 A.M.

Jason frowned, his mind racing. The Silver Spoon was a dive bar nearby, a place he'd been to once or twice when he needed a buzz, or to score some black market Oxys from a guy named Speedy. Not exactly where he expected to find inspiration.

This is bullshit, he thought to himself, cradling the phone in one hand and the fistful of painkillers in the other. *It's got to be. Or a scam. But who knows?* If they were dumb enough to reach out to him, he reasoned, maybe he'd score a free round of drinks at the bar. Jason licked his dry lips.

What did he have to lose?

The dead speak, the message had said. Jason shook his head, trying to dispel the creeping unease that settled over him. *What a crock.* He didn't believe in ghosts or supernatural spirits, but he did believe in a good story. And if this mystery person had a story worth telling, somebody should be there to record it.

What the hell, he shrugged, opening his palm and letting the fistful of pills spill out. *What's one more disappointment?* Yet even as the words echoed in his head, his hope flared out, and Jason closed his eyes, seeking freedom from the agony and the blame, praying for forgiveness, praying for peace. But all he heard from his prayers was silence, and the rattle of pills going down the drain.

CHAPTER THREE

Voices From The Abyss

The dead speak truths the living dare not whisper.

The Silver Spoon was a run-down, broken brick-veneer bar and grill in the decaying part of the city. Jason had strolled down this block a dozen times since moving into his apartment, never seeing any of his neighbors sitting on their porches in the summer heat, fanning themselves to keep the air moving; no children on the neighborhood basketball courts shooting layups; no old men or women paying social calls to their friends — not a single soul was ever on the street. Passing the used car lot, the 24-hour convenience store, the dry cleaners and the abandoned donut shop, Jason wandered to The Silver Spoon, drenched in nervousness. By now it was 6 A.M., another joyless dawn. Drifting past the uncollected garbage, the FOR RENT signs in the yards of the ramshackle houses, Jason's fears began taking root. *So what's the plan? You don't have one, do you?* He hated his helplessness, his inability to control his own life. He'd left his recording gear at home, certain this meeting was a scam, a joke. *Why bother lugging it around?* his tired brain insisted, too sleepy to argue. He could always use the voice memo app installed on his phone, if this stranger even showed up.

Rounding a corner, The Silver Spoon loomed ahead. The sight jarred Jason. *There it is.* He fished in his coat pocket, removed the silver flask of bourbon he'd stuck there, snuck a sip. He hadn't planned on following through on the mysterious message. But maybe drinking at this seedy bar would ease his pain, Jason decided, slipping the flask inside his coat. Maybe the mysterious caller wouldn't show up, and he could sit in the barroom and get hammered, release some of the steam fogging his brain. He thought about turning around and going back home, but facing his blinking laptop screen and the unfinished *Echoes* podcast was the last thing he wanted. So he kept walking.

A minute later he arrived. He stood under the shiny glare of neon, flickering ominously in the pre-dawn darkness. Leaning forward, he looked around. The streets surrounding The Silver Spoon were deserted, the urban city asleep, save for Jason and a few chugging work trucks drifting through the city. Pulling his coat tighter around him, the chill in the air biting through the thin fabric, and feeling a body blow of shame for having any kind of hope that this meeting might lead somewhere, Jason shoved open the creaky door and entered.

Inside, the bar was a tomb — a relic, a forgotten artifact suspended in its own peculiar limbo. The stench of stale beer and cigarette smoke clung to the air like a specter — air that carried a weight, thick and oppressive, pressing against Jason's chest like an unseen hand. Dim overhead lights cast long, distorted shadows that danced across the grimy wooden floor. The flickering neon sign over the bar cast an eerie red glow that pulsed like a heartbeat.

Jason's eyes scanned the room — empty, cracked leather booths, vacant barstools, and an old 45 RPM Wurlitzer jukebox silently gathering dust in the corner. Reflections in the mirrored glass behind the bar seemed warped, bending slightly, distorting shapes in ways that defied explanation. A greasy aroma wafted out from the kitchen. *Too early for the regulars to be boozing it up,* Jason surmised. Not a single customer. Nobody here for breakfast. Nobody sweeping the floor. Not even a bartender in sight.

"Figures," Jason muttered under his breath. Feeling this must be a sign, he cast a frown of betrayal at the room, then turned around to leave.

Then he saw her — a woman seated alone at a darkened corner table, shrouded in an aura of mystery. A wide-brimmed hat concealed much of her face; a long raven-black coat was draped over her shoulders like a cloak. Spying Jason, she lifted a gloved hand, and motioned him over. She seemed out of place, Jason realized, as if she'd stepped out of a different time. Yet something about her pulled at him, a gravitational force he couldn't resist.

As he approached, she lifted her head ever so slightly. Jason was near enough now to see her eyes — the most luminous sea-green eyes Jason had ever seen. Her mouth was wrinkled into a little all-knowing smile. "Jason Marks," she said, her voice low and velvety, tinged with an accent he couldn't place. "The podcaster. You came."

Jason blinked in surprise. Apprehension crept its way up his spine. For a moment he looked back over his shoulder at the doorway, thinking he might hurl himself back out onto the street. Instead, he turned to the woman and smiled as comfortably as he could.

"Yes, that's me," he replied cautiously, pulling out a chair but hesitating before sitting. His palms felt clammy against the worn wood of the table. "And you are...?"

"Elena," she answered simply, her luminous eyes meeting his. She held him with those eyes — eyes that seemed to draw him in, endless pools that hinted at a deeper darkness, at bottomless secrets buried deep.

Jason felt his throat tighten. He finally sat down, but remained perched on the edge of his seat, ready to bolt at any moment. There was a long silence. "So, Elena," he began, forcing a casual smile and a polite tone he didn't feel. "Mind telling me what this is all about? The cryptic messages, the talk of the dead?"

The woman slid her gloved hands across the tabletop. She leaned back in her chair, staring into Jason's face with a look of quiet exasperation. Finally she offered a faint smile. "You're searching for something extraordinary to revive your podcast, aren't you?" Her smile widened, her eyes watching Jason closely. "I can help you."

Jason's eyebrows rose in surprise. Suddenly he wished he'd walked out of the bar; he felt stupid, ridiculous, a fool for holding any hope that this meeting wasn't a scam. He let out a dry laugh. "Right. Sure you can help me. And how exactly do you plan to do that?"

The woman smiled with satisfaction. "By giving you what you seek — the voices of the dead."

He stared at her, trying to read the woman's mind, waiting for the punchline. When none came, he shook his head. "Look, if this is some kind of sick joke —"

"It's no joke," she interrupted, her gaze never wavering. "I can connect you with those who have passed on. They have stories to tell, and you can be the one to share them with the world."

"Connect me with the dead?" Jason scoffed. "That's... absurd."

"Is it?" she challenged softly. "You, of all people, should understand."

Jason's eyes narrowed. Instantly he felt his temples pounding. "What's that supposed to mean?"

Elena leaned forward. When she spoke again, her voice had turned mournful. "You're haunted, Jason. Haunted by loss, by guilt, by a lifetime of questions that have no answers. Your heart has a deep void. You've been searching for something to fill that void."

Jason squinted at the woman. A surge of anger flared within him. "You don't know anything about me," he scoffed, giving her a brazen look.

"I know more than you think," she said calmly. Her glowing eyes bored into his, making Jason's heartbeat quicken. "I know about Judith."

Jason's eyes went glassy. He looked around as if in a dream. *Judith?* Hearing his daughter's name coming from this strange woman hit him like a physical blow. *How does she know about Judith?* Slumping back against his chair, he experienced a dazed sensation pulsing in his head.

"What did you say?" he asked nervously, his heart thumping in his chest, his throat going dry.

"I know Judith," Elena repeated, leaning in and meeting Jason's gaze. "Your deceased daughter."

Jason opened his eyes wide. *Impossible!* his mind screamed. A great, pent-up anger surged inside him. He shot up from his chair, knocking it backward. "Who the hell are you? How do you know about Judith?"

Other than the faint hum of a neon sign, silence enveloped the bar. Elena remained seated, unflinching. "Sit down, Jason."

Sit down? He was shaking with rage. He hesitated, unable to make out her expression under the shadowy brim of her hat. Part of him wanted to storm out, to stagger home to his apartment and drink himself into a stupor; but another part —

a desperate, aching part — needed answers. Slowly, he righted the overturned chair and sat back down, scrutinizing Elena.

"How do you know about Judith?" he demanded.

Elena regarded him thoughtfully. "Because she told me."

Jason gave her a peculiar look. "That's absurd. Impossible."

Elena sat back, tilted her head, keeping her gaze on Jason. "You carry her with you everywhere. The pain, the memories — they're etched into your soul. Judith senses that."

Jason's face darkened. He rubbed his temples, a headache beginning to throb. "This is nuts. It's insane. *You're* insane."

"Perhaps," she conceded. "But that doesn't make it any less real."

Jason exhaled sharply. He paused for a long moment before he spoke, thoughts racing through his skull. There was no part of him that believed this was happening. "Alright, let's say — for the sake of argument — that I believe you can do what you claim. What's in it for you?"

Elena leaned forward. "Closure," she said simply. "For them, and perhaps for you as well."

Them? Who is them? Jason wondered. He studied her, searching for any sign of deception. "And you just want to help me out of the kindness of your heart?"

"I have my reasons," she replied enigmatically. "But time is short, Jason. The veil between worlds is thin, and the voices grow restless."

Jason smirked, sat back, crossing his arms defensively. He didn't have a clue how this woman knew about Judith. For a moment he saw his daughter lying on a steel gurney in the city morgue, covered by a white sheet. Shocked by this memory, his throat closed up, pain worming a path down his chest.

Elena's gloved hands rested lightly on the tabletop. She smiled faintly, wryly. "Are you ready?"

Jason hesitated. Was he ready? The answer didn't matter. "Assuming I go along with this," he said to Elena, noticing the small crack in his voice, "how does it work?"

A hint of a smile played on her lips. "You let me guide you. Open your mind to the possibilities. Record the dead's stories, share them. And in doing so, perhaps find some peace."

Find some peace? Jason stared at Elena, afraid he'd said the words out loud. He shook his head. "This is... I don't know..."

Yes, you do know! Jason's thoughts shrieked. *Record the dead? You're being a fool!*

Again Elena narrowed her eyes at Jason. Her smile froze. She reached into her coat pocket and pulled out a small, intricately carved wooden box. She placed it gently on the table. "Sometimes," she said, "seeing is believing."

Jason eyed the box warily. It sat between them, its surface catching faint glimmers of light that seemed to dance along its edges. There was a long, cold silence. "What's that?"

"A conduit," she explained. "A way to bridge the gap."

In Jason's mind everything slowed to a crawl. *Bridge the gap? What does that mean?* He tried to take a deep breath, but his lungs felt constricted. *Bridge the gap between life and death?* The words sank in, and the world around Jason receded.

He hesitated, then slowly reached out to touch the box. The wood felt warm under his fingertips, almost pulsing with life, with energy. Still the idea of speaking with the dead seemed ridiculous. *Yet what if one could?* Jason wondered — and in his wondering, felt a stirring in his soul, a premonition.

"What do I do?" he asked.

"Start recording. Then close your eyes," Elena instructed softly. "Focus on the sound of my voice."

Jason did not reply. Against his better judgment, he complied. He bent down into his pocket. Fumbling to pull out his cellphone, he scrolled clumsily through screen after screen, finally punching in the voice memo app. Hitting the red RECORD button, he gently closed his eyes. The darkness behind his eyelids was a welcome respite from her penetrating gaze.

"Take a deep breath," Elena continued. "Clear your mind. Let go of doubt. And *listen…*"

Jason inhaled slowly, the scent of sandalwood and something else — something ancient — filling his senses. He waited. And waited. Nothing was happening. He tilted his chin up, took a deeper breath, let it out. Still nothing.

"Think of Judith," Elena said.

A knot formed in Jason's stomach. "I can't."

"Yes, you can. Remember her laugh, her smile, the way she held your hand."

Shutting his eyes tighter Jason leaned forward, resisting the urge to open them. Suddenly the hum of the room died; a bright light flooded his vision. Images going back years formed in front of him: Judith chasing butterflies in the park, her face smeared with chocolate ice cream, her eyes lighting up when he read her favorite bedtime story, *Green Eggs and Ham*.

"Good," Elena's voice seemed to come from a distance. "Now, Jason. Listen."

Jason listened. At first, there was nothing. Then, ever so softly, he heard it, a trickle of gentle sound, echoing from across the table, coming from Elena's seat — a child's giggle, light and free and airy.

His eyes snapped open. "What was that?"

Elena's eyes remained closed. Jason tilted his head, startled — the laughing voice was obviously coming from her. But how?

Immediately the air seemed to shift, growing heavier, colder. A hum vibrated at the edges of Jason's hearing, so low it might have been imagined. Shadows deepened, the light in the barroom dimming until it felt like the world had been wrapped in a gray unearthly haze.

Jason shivered as the temperature dropped. His breath misted in front of him, and he rubbed his hands together, thinking for a moment about pulling the flask of bourbon out of his pocket to warm him.

"Keep listening," Elena gently interrupted.

Jason closed his eyes again, waiting, straining to hear. Softly the giggle came again, closer to Jason this time. *Is it some parlor trick?* he wondered. *Yet it couldn't be!* The laughter he heard was embedded in his memory, the details of the voice so clear to him, as if locked away in a time capsule.

"…Daddy?"

His heart lurched. *That voice — no — dear God, it couldn't be! Could it…?*

"Daddy, it's me…Judith."

Jason's shock melted away. Without realizing it, he smiled. He wanted to reach out, and touch this voice. *I hear you, Judith. I hear you!* Tears welled up, spilling desperately down his cheeks. "Judith?" he choked out.

"I'm here, Daddy," the voice continued, familiar and clearer now, resonating within him. "I sure have missed you."

Jason was hit by a wave of dizziness. He clutched the edge of the table, fingers clenched, knuckles white. "This isn't real. It *can't* be."

"I've been watching over you," she said softly. "I'm sorry I had to leave."

Leave? Jason laughed; she hadn't left him! Reflexively he reached up to touch the warm embrace. Memories from the past washed over him — there he was, in his pajamas and robe seated in his favorite chair in their home, drinking coffee and reading the newspaper. And here came Judith, leaping into his lap, coffee spilling everywhere, the world screeching to a halt as he laughed and hugged her. Kissing his cheek, Judith handed Jason a note she'd scribbled in purple crayon. Jason opened it: THANK YOU AND MOMMY FOR MAKING ME! the note read. Lowering his head now, Jason sobbed. And then another memory rushed to him. And another. And another —

Emotion crashed over him like a tidal wave. "No, *I'm* sorry," he sobbed to Judith. "I should have —"

"It's not your fault," Judith interrupted gently. "Really, Daddy. But now you need to let me go."

Let you go? Jason shook his head violently. "I *can't*. I don't know how!"

"Let me help you," she pleaded.

He felt a warmth envelop him, a sensation of tiny arms wrapping around his neck in a familiar and loving embrace. *Dear God, what a beautiful feeling!* he thought, leaning back in his chair, pleading with this embrace not to float away.

"Do you remember Winston?" the voice asked.

Jason froze. "Winston?"

"Our cat," Judith reminded him. "Winston's here. He keeps me company."

A laugh bubbled up through his tears. "Winston hated everyone. Everyone but you."

Judith giggled. "He's still grumpy."

Jason smiled despite himself, the ache in his chest easing ever so slightly. "Judith, I — "

"Shhh," she soothed. "It's okay, Daddy. You don't have to say anything."

Jason sat there, eyes closed, basking in the ephemeral connection, wishing it could last forever. A way for father and daughter to never be apart. Even if it was only a voice in his mind…

"Time's almost up," she whispered. "But I'll always be with you."

"Don't go!" he begged.

"I'll be here when you need me," she promised. "And Harold, my stuffed teddy bear, is still down there, watching over you. But you have to go live your life."

Jason tried to speak, his chest fluttering. Suddenly the warmth of embrace he'd felt began to fade, the voice growing distant.

"*Judith!!*" Jason cried out.

Silence.

He opened his eyes, gasping as if he'd surfaced from deep underwater. Elena was coming out of her trance, shaking her head as if to clear it. Leaning back in her chair, she watched Jason intently, a mixture of empathy and exhaustion etched on her face.

"How... how is this possible?" he stammered.

Elena smiled. She could see Jason's eyes were damp and shining, filled with questions, and with love. She gave a small nod. "There are more things in Heaven and earth than are dreamt of in your philosophy."

Jason wiped his eyes with the back of his hand. All at once there was something new in his heart. *Hope. There's hope.* He looked directly in Elena's face. "Why me? Why help me?"

"Because you needed it," she replied. "And because you can help others."

He sat in stunned silence, hands trembling, the weight of what had he had just experienced settling over him. "What happens now?"

"Now," she said, her tone turning businesslike, "we give others the chance to tell their stories. You record them, share them. Help them find peace, and perhaps find some yourself."

Jason glanced at his phone, the voice memo app still recording. "This is... it's unbelievable."

"Believe it," Elena said firmly. "Are you ready to begin?"

He took a deep breath, considering the path laid out before him. It was insanity, it was madness, yes, but maybe a kind of madness he needed.

"Who... who do we start with?" he asked cautiously.

Elena's eyes sparkled. "There's a painter who's been waiting a long time to set the record straight. His story has been misunderstood for over a century."

"A painter?" Jason's heart stopped in his chest.

She smiled enigmatically. "His name is Vincent."

Silently Jason gazed at her. Once again he felt the tears springing to his eyes. "Vincent," he repeated, a tingle of anticipation mixing with lingering disbelief. "As in van Gogh?"

"Precisely," she confirmed. "He's eager to talk."

Jason looked down at his phone; it was still recording. He nodded, picked it up, checking the battery life. His hands were steadier now, a sense of purpose beginning to take root.

"Okay," he said, meeting her gaze. "I'm in."

Elena nodded approvingly. "Very well." She closed her eyes once more, her features relaxing into a serene mask. Again she rested her hands on the wooden box. Concentrating. Focusing.

The air grew thick, the ambient sounds fading into the background. When she spoke again, her voice carried a different timbre, accented and rich with emotion.

"Hello, Jason. My name is Vincent...Vincent van Gogh. I've been waiting for someone to listen."

Jason felt a chill run down his spine, a pounding in his chest. *What in heaven have I gotten myself into?* Without missing a beat, he hit SAVE on the current recording and started a new one. He drew a breath, let it out, and noticed the trembling in his hands had stopped.

"I'm listening," he said quietly.

As the words flowed from Elena's — *no, Vincent's* — lips, Jason realized that his life had irrevocably changed. The abyss he'd been teetering over didn't seem so deep anymore. For the first time in years, he felt connected — not just to the living, but to the tapestry of stories that bound all souls together. He leaned forward, phone in hand, ready to capture the echoes of the past.

"Tell me everything," he whispered.

And so the dead began to speak.

CHAPTER FOUR

The Dead Speak

Art bleeds colors the world cannot contain.

Again the air in the barroom seemed to shift, as if whirlpooling around Jason, charged with an invisible cosmic energy. Jason sat back, stunned. He felt a rushing cold envelop him, an icelike breath surrounding him; the feeling was unshakable. *What's happening?* he wondered, in a panic. *Where had this icy touch come from?* He looked at Elena — she sat silently across the table from him, her eyes closed, serene and peaceful, her body still as she channeled the spirit of Vincent van Gogh.

Suddenly the rays of the morning sun broke through the windows of The Silver Spoon. Now there was warmth, beams of a dawning fireball rising in the west, and the heat of the golden sunshine melted the icy cold that surrounded Jason.

The air pulsed and shifted again. Soundless energy swirling as if from the box at Elena's fingertips. Jason looked around with amazement. Over his shoulder he was surprised to see the bartender, cleaning beer glasses with a towel, wiping down the bar as if nothing had happened.

Get hold of yourself, his mind commanded Jason. *If you're going to speak with the dead, then talk. Start talking.*

Jason leaned forward, heart pounding. He cleared his throat, his voice shaking as he began.

"Vincent…can…can you hear me?"

There was no reply. Only silence. Jason leaned in closer, worried he'd lost the connection.

"Vincent, are you there? Can you *hear* me?" he begged.

Again there was silence. Jason's throat tightened. He reached down and slid the recorder near the box, in an act of desperation, hoping and praying this might help, then he lifted his eyes up to Elena — and a fearsome look covered his face.

Elena was struggling, quivering. She lurched backward into her seat, eyes clenched tight, jawbone jutted out, her face hidden in the gloom under the brim of her hat. She plunged her head down, perhaps digging deeper into whatever supernatural force she commanded, into whatever she channeled to touch and reach the dead.

Jason sat frozen. His face drained. Elena opened her lips, but no words came out. *What's the matter?* Jason wondered, and for one wild, terrible moment that nauseating feeling of hopelessness returned. Elena's breathing slowed, her body stiffening as if she were bracing against an unseen force. Then, with a shudder, she tilted her head back, her lips parting — and a soothing, gentle, far-off voice cut through the fog of confusion.

"Yes, Jason, I can hear you," came the reply. The voice, resonant with a refined Dutch accent, carried the weight of long lonely years spent in isolation, in grief and inner turmoil — yet it was a steady voice, calm. A voice that had found the doorway to peace. "This is Vincent. I'm here with you."

Suddenly Jason felt like laughing. The flutter in his chest stopped. He composed himself. *I can't believe this is really happening!* He barely noticed Elena now; his mind was consumed with anticipation, with a rush of emotions, eager to speak with the legendary painter, an artist he'd worshipped, who'd haunted his thoughts for years until van Gogh had become a kindred spirit, an invisible coping mechanism for his own pain and struggles.

My lifelong dream! What should I ask? Quickly his thoughts went blank, swallowed up into an empty abyss of nervousness. This wasn't just another interview — it was the opportunity of a lifetime to delve into the soul of a man whose life and work had carried Jason through his darkest moments, who had become an obsession.

As a boy, Jason had fantasized what this would be like, meeting van Gogh. He had dreamed of this moment for years, had imagined a hundred different questions, but now his thoughts felt scattered, his heart pounding too loudly to focus.

He blinked back tears of joy. Excavating those boyhood memories now, he began rolling out questions.

"Vincent, I...I can't believe we're finally speaking..." he stammered. "It's an unbelievable honor. Your work has touched so many hearts, so many lives — especially mine," he smiled — and suddenly realized his hands were clutched tight to the edge of the table, his knuckles whitening. "Let me ask you something: during your life, you faced rejection constantly, your art always underappreciated, unrecognized, misunderstood. How on earth did you cope with that?"

A pause followed. Instantly Jason's smile was erased. When Vincent spoke again, his voice was reflective, almost melancholic.

"I poured my heart and soul into my work, my art, my paintings. And in the process, I lost myself, my way, my mind. I allowed the opinions of others to choke and strangle me in self-doubt. And because of this, the world often seemed cold and indifferent. To create was to suffer, to undergo cruel punishment — yet creating was also my only deliverance. My salvation." From faraway Jason heard Vincent's dark chuckle. "Isn't it strange, Jason? How something that brings so much pain into lives like yours and mine can also be our greatest source of hope and strength?"

Jason stared, astounded. *How did he know about my pain?* He shook it off, then turned his eyes back to Elena. Elena was calm now, eyes shut, sitting rock solid in her chair, the dark energy gone. She seemed no longer to be suffering in the throes of connecting with the dead, with this strange and mystical encounter.

Where did this woman come from? Jason thought to himself. *And what pain is she putting herself through?* With a shrug, Jason decided it didn't matter. Elena was proving her abilities. *My God, this woman really can channel the dead! It's undeniable! More than that,* Jason perceived, *it's a miracle!*

Putting his shock aside, Jason returned to his interview.

"Let's talk about your letters. You once wrote to your brother Theo, saying, 'What am I in the eyes of most people? A nonentity, an eccentric, or an unpleasant person — somebody who has no position in society and never will have; in short, the lowest of the low.' Vincent, how did you deal with that feeling of unworthiness?"

Vincent's voice grew somber, heavy with the weight of the past. "I remember those words well. There were many nights when the darkness seemed impenetrable, impassable, and I wondered if my efforts to paint and touch others were in vain. But I believed in the power of art to transcend my own life's limitations. I clung to the hope that one day, someone would see the light in my work. It was a desperate hope, but it kept me going."

Jason nodded, thinking to himself, staring into the mirrored glass behind the bar. "The greatest tragedy is not in being misunderstood, Jason," Vincent continued, "but in never being heard at all, never seen, your most soulful work tossed aside, as if it were a piece of garbage."

Across the table Jason heard a whimpering sound. Looking at Elena, tears leaking from her clenched eyes, he realized Vincent himself was sobbing. Again the icy cold enveloped Jason. *My God, even the dead can feel pain!*

As the thought struck him, all at once Jason experienced a wave of incredible agony. Jolts of emotions — rejection, disappointment, anguish, heartache — exploded in his brain. He gasped out, suddenly whipping his hands up to his temples. Cold sweat beaded on his face; tears rolled out of his eyes. Gazing down, he saw his fists clenched into tight balls, the knuckles bloodless and white.

Is this what it's like to be van Gogh? he almost screamed out. *A tortured artist, trying desperately to connect with his audience? To be dead for a century, body turned to ashes, buried in a grave, and still experience earthbound emotions — grief, regret, shame, loneliness?*

"Do you feel it now, Jason?" van Gogh said, his voice cracking with sorrow. "My pain? To know that the world has turned its back on you? You feel this also in your life, I know."

Jason tried to relax his clenched fists, his throat dry. "Yes," he answered, flexing his aching fingers. "I do."

"That is the pain I also feel. Not the insanity, or the madness people talk about. Not the hunger for success, adoration, or the loneliness. It's the *silence.* The silence after you've shouted your truth to the world, and no one listens…"

"You understand me, Jason," van Gogh said, his voice sounding crushed. "Perhaps in a way no other human being ever has."

Jason wiped away his tears with the back of his hand. He shook his head, confusion drizzling through him. *Can't stop to think about this. Can't dissect and analyze this*, his mind warned him. *Just keep going. Don't stop now. Now is your one chance to really experience something unheard of.* Swiping away the sweat he leaned forward and continued.

"In another letter to Theo, you said, 'If you hear a voice within you say, "You cannot paint," then by all means paint, and that voice will be silenced.' You seemed to have pushed through self-doubt with a kind of superhuman perseverance, a relentless tenacity. How did you manage to keep going, even when that voice of self-sabotage screamed to stop you?"

Vincent's tone softened, a quiet resolve in his words. "That voice is the enemy of every artist. It whispers doubts and fears, it whispers warnings of failure — but it must be confronted. I found that the act of painting itself could silence that voice, by creating. Painting, sketching, a brush in my hand, I could overcome those internal barriers. I could translate my inner pain into something the world could see. Perseverance, even in the face of self-doubt, was the only way forward. Each brushstroke was a defiance against that voice, a declaration that I would not be silenced…

"Besides," he said, "without art, without using whatever gift God gave each of us, what purpose is there in life? We both have struggled with feelings of purposelessness, have we not?"

There he goes again! Jason sat bolt upright in his chair, startled. *How does this dead man know of my struggles? Did Judith tell him?* For a moment, Jason considered this outrageous thought, letting it sink in. *Could it be Judith? My daughter? No,* his brain scoffed, *that's not possible!...Or is it?*

And yet, the words van Gogh spoke about rejection and isolation, purposelessness and unworthiness, haunted him. Hearing the man speak now, it felt like van Gogh's ghost had taken up residence inside Jason. The idea made him flinch. He understood what Vincent meant about punishment. *Echoes,* his podcast, had begun to feel less like a creative outlet, and more like self-punishment, a curse, a burden.

Just then — before Jason realized what he was seeing — he caught a glimpse of Elena. Eyes scrunched tighter than ever, her body swayed in her seat, moaning as the power of channeling Vincent surged through her.

Realizing their time might be running short, Jason returned briskly to their interview.

"Vincent, you also wrote, 'I want to touch people with my art. I want them to say, "van Gogh feels deeply, he feels tenderly."' It seems that you saw art as more than just a personal expression — it was a way to connect with others on an emotional level, perhaps even a level of spirit. Can you tell me more about that?"

Vincent's voice took on a reflective tone, as if he were searching for the right words. "Art, to me, was always about communication. It was a way to convey what was locked away in my heart, to reach out to others and say, 'I understand you, and I want you to understand me.' I wanted people to feel the tenderness, the love, the depth of emotion that I felt when I painted. It was never just about the image — never, Jason! It was about the feeling behind the image. The connection it could create between me and the viewer. That was the true meaning of art for me."

Jason could feel the sincerity in Vincent's voice. *Dig deeper,* he told himself. *Ask another question, take a chance.* "Yet you never accomplished this connection during your lifetime. You described yourself as 'an eccentric, a nobody.' You also said, 'I should one day like to show by my work what such an eccentric, such a nobody, has in his heart.' It sounds like you embraced your suffering and your passion as integral to your creative process. How did you reconcile the two?"

Vincent's voice darkened. "Suffering and passion were intertwined for me, Jason. My suffering gave birth to my passion, and my passion fueled and inflamed my art. I believed that through my pain, my agony, I could create something that resonated with others, something that spoke to the human condition. I wanted to show that even a nobody could have something important to say, something that could touch others' hearts. My art was my way of transforming that suffering into something beautiful, something meaningful."

Jason was silent for a moment, letting Vincent's words sink in. He decided to attempt a new direction. "Let me ask you something else. You once said, 'If one truly loves nature, one finds beauty everywhere.' Your work often reflects a deep connection to nature. How did nature inspire you? How did it influence your art?"

Vincent's voice brightened, as if recalling moments of peace amidst the chaos. "Nature was my refuge, my sanctuary. It was in the fields, the forests, the changing skies that I found solace and inspiration. There was a purity in nature, a simplicity that I could not find anywhere else. In those moments, surrounded by the beauty of the natural world, I felt closest to something divine. I wanted to capture that beauty, that sense of wonder, that childlike innocence in my paintings — *The Starry Night*, *The Bedroom*, and especially *Sunflowers*. In my time, Jason, the sunflowers spoke to me. Their withering petals were more honest than the eyes of any man." For a moment, van Gogh paused; Jason bit his tongue to keep from saying, *Keep going, Vincent, keep going.* "Nature was not just a subject for me — it was a source of inspiration, a guide that taught me how to see the world with fresh eyes."

Jason cast a worried glance over at Elena, ready to drop to his knees and beg her to keep this connection with van Gogh open, no matter what it cost her. *Hurry, Jason,* his brain warned him. He hurried. "You also said, 'The more I think it over, the more I feel that there is nothing more truly artistic than to love people.' It seems like your work was deeply connected to your love for humanity. How did that love shape your role as an artist?"

"For me, the highest calling of an artist was to express love for humanity. My work was a reflection of that love, a way to show that even in the midst of suffering, there is beauty, there is hope. I wanted my art to be a bridge between people, to foster connection and understanding. To love much is to give much, and though I received little in return, the act of giving was enough. My art was my way of loving the world, even when it seemed unlovable."

Jason felt a lump in his throat. The depth of Vincent's love, his capacity to give despite everything, despite the anguish, despite the world's punishment, was overwhelming. Jason fought back tears, thinking of his own unrequited love. "But Vincent, it must have been so painful to give so much and receive so little in return! Didn't that make the loneliness even harder to bear?"

Vincent's voice trembled. "Ah, yes, the loneliness. The loneliness was unbearable. There were days when I felt like I was screaming and howling into the void — and the only response was silence. But I also knew that the pain was a necessary part of the process. To create, one must be willing to suffer, to dig deep into the soul and confront the darkness within. My art was born out of that struggle, out of the need to find light in the midst of darkness. Without it, Jason, I would have been lost."

The word *darkness* slammed through Jason, the rawness of the word cutting through the silence. "Let's talk about the darkness. You once described your mind as 'like a night full of fire.' How did you manage to keep going, even when the fire threatened to consume you?"

Vincent's voice grew more intense, as if reliving the anguish. "The fire inside me was both a blessing and an eternal damnation, a curse. It fueled my creativity, gave me the energy to keep painting, even when I was on the brink of despair. But it also threatened to destroy me, to consume everything in its path, like an unholy wildfire. I often felt like I was walking a tightrope, balancing between creation and destruction. There were days when the fire burned too brightly, and I feared it would consume me. But I had no choice but to keep going, to channel that fire into my work. It was the only way I knew how to survive."

Jason nodded. The struggle Vincent described resonated deeply, a battle between creation and destruction that he too had often faced. "And yet," Jason persisted, "despite everything, you never gave up. What kept you striving, even when the world seemed so against you?"

"It was that search for beauty, for meaning, that kept me going. Do you know the tragedy of the artist, my friend? It is to see the world not as it is, but as it *could* be, and to be punished for daring to dream. I believed that if I could capture just a fraction of the beauty I saw in the world, it would be enough. I often told Theo that I felt like a pilgrim, wandering through life in search of something greater, something beyond myself. My art was my way of reaching for that. I knew I might never find it, but I could not stop searching. To stop would have been to admit defeat, and that was something I could not do."

Jason remained silent, letting Vincent's words sink in. The intensity of the artist's passion, his unwavering commitment to his work, was both inspiring and heartbreaking. Returning to his own heartbreak, he thought of Judith, her laughter, her absence, the way his grief had swallowed him whole. He thought of his podcast, *Echoes,* the stories he'd tried to tell, the voices he'd tried to amplify. Was he any different?

"You talk like there's some grand design to all this suffering," Jason said, feeling a gnawing need to confront his own chaotic life. "What about the people who just…fail? Who never find their way?"

"Do you truly believe failure is the end?" Vincent asked. "It is only the silence between one note and the next, a rest in the music of the soul."

Jason sat very still, troubled by the enigma of Vincent's starry-eyed words. "You think creating is some kind of cure-all," he scoffed. "But it's just another way to be rejected. Look at me — no one listens, no one cares!"

"Then you are fortunate, Jason. Rejection is the fire that tempers the steel. It is in obscurity that the artist finds the purity of their voice."

"But what you're saying seems impenetrable! I need simple answers!"

There was a silence. "You want simple, Jason? I see the

answer in your eyes. The same despair that darkened my nights in Arles. Tell me, what shadow weighs on your soul?"

Jason hung his miserable head. "You wouldn't understand. Nobody does. It's not just about being unheard — it's about being *unseen*. Like I'm screaming into a void. You make everything sound so easy, like pain is just fuel for art. But what if I have nothing left to give?"

"You have your *voice,* Jason. Even in the depths of silence, you are never truly empty. Speak, and let the echoes remind you of who you are."

Neither one said anything. Jason looked back at Elena, her head swaying gently, eyes moving under her eyelids in psychic connection. He pressed on to the next question.

"Vincent," he said hesitantly, "what would you have done differently? If you had another chance?"

"I would have painted one more masterpiece," van Gogh softly replied. "A final canvas to say what words and colors alone never could. But life is cruel, Jason. It takes before you are ready to give."

The words struck something deep within Jason. He looked to his left, and saw the bartender standing in the kitchen doorway, curiously eyeing he and Elena. To his right Jason could hear her breath, her soft moaning in deep concentration. *Wonder what that old guy's thinking?* he pondered, and then his mind darted back to the conversation. "Your relationship with your brother Theo was foundational to your life and work. How important was that support, and how did it influence your courage to keep going?"

Vincent's voice grew tender. "Theo was my anchor, my lifeline. Without Theo's support, his inextinguishable love for me, his brother, I would not have had the courage to pursue my art, to keep going in the face of so much adversity. Theo believed in me when no one else did, and that belief gave me the strength to attempt the impossible. Life requires courage, Jason, the courage to face our fears, to take risks, to put ourselves out there even when we are afraid of failing. Theo's support was a reminder that I was not alone, that I had someone in my corner who believed in me. That made all the difference."

"You also said," Jason continued, "'The sadness will last forever.' These were reportedly your last words. Do you still feel that sadness, even now?"

There was a long silence, and when Vincent spoke, his voice was filled with profound resignation. "Yes, Jason, the sadness does last forever. It is a part of who I am. But I have learned to live with it, to accept it as a companion on this journey. The sadness is not something to be feared, but something to be understood. It is a reminder of life's fragility, of the splendor of divine love that can be found even in the bleakest moments. I believe it is through our sadness, our suffering, that we find our greatest strength, our deepest connections with others."

Jason felt tears streaming down his face, the raw emotion in Vincent's words cutting deep. He pictured his own life, his hopeless situation, his cramped, rat-filled apartment. "Vincent, what advice would you give to someone who is struggling, who feels lost in the darkness?"

Vincent's voice grew tender, filled with compassion. "In the depths of despair, it is easy to believe there is no way out, that the darkness will never end. But in those moments, we must hold on to the things that bring us joy, that give our lives meaning. For me, it was painting. For others, it might be music, writing, or simply caring for another. We must not let the world's indifference rob us of our will to create, to love, to live. It is through these acts of creation that we find our way back to the light."

The light. He keeps talking about the light. Yet van Gogh's life was a life trapped under a cloud of anguish. Jason paused, thinking of the one thing he hadn't asked in this interview. The one thing he'd never understood, even as a boy worshipping this great artist. He had to ask. Now.

"Vincent, let me ask you about 1888."

"Yes, Jason."

"On the night before Christmas Eve, 1888, during what's been described as a mental health crisis, a breakdown, you famously sliced off part of your left ear, after an argument with the artist Paul Gauguin." For a moment Jason's voice froze. He hated to ask. *But I must go there. I must know!* He needed to probe, to discover a deeper understanding. "Why, Vincent? Why did you do it?"

There was a pause. A thick, heavy silence.

"Please, Vincent, help me to understand," Jason begged.

"It wasn't about Paul Gauguin," Vincent answered. "It was about Theo."

"Theo?"

"I cut off my ear after learning my brother Theo was getting married. I feared being abandoned, rejected again…Theo and I were so close! And his engagement pushed my heart over the edge. Suddenly I felt alone, no one there to hear my pain. Was I alone? Perhaps. Was it a mistake to give up on life? Yes, Jason. It was. But I always believed in another world, a heavenly place, a better world somewhere."

Jason looked again at the window, at the blinding rays of the morning sun, beams slashing through the grimy barroom. "Is there, Vincent?" he asked uneasily. "Is there a better world?"

Before van Gogh could answer, Jason felt something in the room shifting, changing. Icy air rushed over him again, swirling around his shoulders. *Time to end now,* he realized, jolted into a panic, that fluttering of dread returning, *before we're cut off.*

"Vincent," Jason began, his voice struggling to remain steady, "there may be young people listening who might be going through a rough patch in their lives. They look up to figures like you, not just for your art, but for the resilience you showed in the face of never-ending adversity. What message would you like to share with them?"

"What message?" There was a pause. When the voice of van Gogh finally spoke, it was filled with peace.

"Life is not an easy road. There will be times when the darkness seems all-consuming, when it feels like the world has turned its back on you. In those moments, it is easy to lose hope, to believe there is no light at the end of the tunnel. Always my thoughts return to the light. For the light is always there, even if it is difficult to see. It may be a faint glimmer, a distant star, but it exists within each of us. That light is our passion for living, our capacity to love and care for others."

Vincent's voice grew softer, filled with urgency. "I have known great sorrow and faced many dark nights of the soul. But I have also known the joy that comes from creating, from pouring one's heart into something that matters. I want young people to understand that they are not alone in their struggles. We all carry our burdens, our fears, but it is in the act of persevering, of continuing to create, to love, that we find our true strength…

"Hold on to that light, no matter how small it may seem," Vincent continued. "Tell them to keep creating, keep dreaming, keep loving. The world may not always understand them, but that does not diminish their worth. Each of them has something unique to offer, something that no one else can give. They must believe in that, even when it feels like no one else does. And remember, the darkest nights often produce the brightest stars."

Jason was silent, the glimmer of Vincent's words settling over him like a warm blanket. It was a message of resilience, and the importance of holding on, even when the road ahead seemed uncertain.

"Thank you, Vincent," Jason said, his voice thick with emotion. "I will make sure your message reaches them."

The voice of Vincent softened, a note of finality in its tone. "Thank you, Jason, for listening. Thank you for giving voice to us."

As the connection began to fade, the room shifted again. The light in the barroom dimmed, flickering unnaturally, and the temperature plunged. Jason felt the icy grip return, tightening around his chest. He gasped, clutching the table as the air seemed to swirl, shapes around Jason coiling and unwinding, the air emitting its own light, an iridescent green that didn't belong in this world.

"Vincent, wait!" he cried, panic rising in his throat.

But it was too late. The cosmic energy had vanished, returning to something more grounded. Letting out a sigh Jason sat back, the weight of the conversation hanging over him. He had expected to hear about Vincent's struggles and pain, but he hadn't anticipated the profound connection he now felt — to van Gogh, to his own creative work, and to the countless others who had ever felt lost in the dark.

Plucking up his cellphone, Jason checked his recording, pressed the SAVE button. Before doing anything else he sent a safety copy to his email address. Then he sat and picked at the phone with his fingernail.

He remained very still, sitting with his arms on the tabletop and looking down at his shoes. Stunned, he raised his head and stared around. Saw the bartender had disappeared. The barroom still empty. Jukebox silent. Nobody drinking at the bar. Nobody out on the street. Not a soul in sight.

As he placed his phone in his pocket, Jason's thoughts raced. He had a story now — a story that might not only save his podcast, but also touch the hearts of those who needed it most. Buttoning his coat he stood. Vincent's words still echoed in his mind, and he couldn't shake the feeling that he had just opened a door that could never be closed.

But perhaps, he thought, that was the point.

That door could never have opened without Elena. Hours ago, Jason had been filled with the blackest despair. Now he wanted desperately to thank her, to embrace her, to express his gratitude to this strange and gifted woman who'd changed his life, given him hope — burning hope! — and taken his wildest dreams to a place he'd never imagined.

But when he turned to thank her, Elena was gone. The chair where she'd sat was empty, the faint indentation on the leather the only sign she had ever been there at all.

* * *

The rain started as Jason walked home. Arriving at his apartment, he stood at the window and watched the storm pound the city, the cloudy skies churning black. Cars on the street, their windshield wipers thrashing back and forth, pulled to the curb, nervous drivers unable to see the path ahead through the downpour. Homeless people scattered, running for shelter as thunder boomed and lightning crashed.

As he watched, Jason's thoughts returned to something van Gogh had said. *A glimpse of the world as it truly is. But some truths are too heavy for human hands to hold.* He reflected on this. Then Jason went to his laptop to record an opening monologue for the podcast.

"Vincent van Gogh once said that great things are not done by impulse, but by a series of small things brought together. Perhaps this podcast is my small thing. Perhaps my voice, insignificant as it feels, is the beginning of something greater. For those of you listening tonight…let the echoes remind you that in the darkness there is light."

Pressing SAVE on the recording, Jason closed his laptop. Suddenly he was reminded of something else the famous painter had mentioned. *A canvas he kept hidden from the world, not ready for their eyes.* He returned to the window. The skies outside weren't black and stormy anymore; they'd turned a bright blue, the rain washed away. The city was splashed with color — brick walls radiated burnt sienna, and streetlights shimmered with gold leaf. Jason saw beauty everywhere; yet it felt borrowed, as if Vincent had lent him his eyes to see.

What if there's more, he pondered, *not just after death, but now, right now? What if I've spent all this time surviving, when I should've been creating?*

Turning from the window, Jason's breath caught in his throat. With a smile he crossed the room, and went to rummage in the closet. From deep inside, he dragged out a dusty painting canvas, one he'd abandoned years ago. The canvas was brittle with age, half-formed lines mocking him. Going to the desk, Jason fished around for his old drawing pencil. *Perhaps if I just start, it will come together,* he told himself, feeling a tremble of something he'd lost now reawakening. Then slowly, letting the pencil lead him, Jason began sketching again, each stroke tentative but filled with a new sense of purpose.

CHAPTER FIVE

Lost in a Dream

Fame devours its children in precise increments.

At the stroke of 9 o'clock P.M. Jason placed his sketch back inside the closet. His hands and his arms ached from the hours of intense sketching. That night — restless, emotionally drained, his entire body drenched in a cold sweat — he lay in bed in his apartment, his hands trembling, his feverish mind trying to sort out the strangeness of his interview with van Gogh.

Go to sleep, he told his anxious brain, while his heart thudded. *Stop worrying. What are you so panicked about?* But Jason's heart would not stop; his mind would not settle. In his dizziness he imagined the faint scent of turpentine and earth clung to his bed clothes, as if Vincent had crawled from the grave and followed him home. The bizarre meeting with Elena, speaking with the dead spirit of his idol — all of it had shaken Jason to his core. Nestled under the sheets his body shivered, perspiration streaming from his every pore. With the door locked and the curtains shut, the outside world blocked from Jason's ready-to-implode senses, his apartment was without the faintest ray of light — for it was in the dark tonight that Jason felt oddly sheltered, protected, safe.

And more than safe — for wide awake in the dark, he could lie quietly and see his dream coming to life; he could fantasize.

In his mind, the response to his first episode with the dead van Gogh would be nothing short of explosive, astounding, a media sensation. The number of listeners to *Echoes* would skyrocket overnight, his inbox flooded with emails from adoring fans who were both enthralled and shocked into senselessness by what they had heard. The Vincent episode would go viral, would be discussed on internet forums, social media, and even mainstream TV news outlets. No longer would *Echoes* be just another struggling podcast, and he — its host, its creator — unknown; both would become absolute phenomenons.

But the more Jason's brain spun beautiful visions of the future, visions that calmed him, and soothed him, the more this future success gnawed at him — for with it came an unexpected burden. The voice of Vincent, so filled with sorrow, grief and regret, murmuring of a lifetime of isolation and rejection, haunted him long after the morning's interview had ended. Jason couldn't shake the feeling that he had touched something profound, something unearthly, something that perhaps shouldn't be touched or unearthed…and it had left a mark on him. And now, if he was a success, he would be required to dive back into that world, again and again, into communicating with the realm of the dead.

Jason hadn't considered this. *Speaking with the dead, the departed, with ghosts. What unholy force am I tapping into?* he breathlessly worried. All night long, the words Vincent spoke during their interview echoed in Jason's mind; in the darkness, it felt like van Gogh's ghost had taken up residence inside him.

There was a clock by his bedside, reading 3:51 A.M. *Is that all it is?* It seemed like hours ago that Jason had posted the new episode on his website. He turned to the cool side of his pillow, and lay still, eyes wide and concentrating on the ceiling, his pulse racing. He couldn't wait to see the new podcast listener numbers; waiting all night to see the numbers set his teeth on edge. Rolling over, he lay flat on his stomach, and listened to the wind rip and rattle the bedroom window. Then he rolled to his side, and faced the cracked apartment wall, replaying the events of the morning.

Clutching his cellphone, he'd come tearing out of The Silver Spoon, in a spellbound rush to race through the rain to his apartment. The sooner he left Elena, and was breathing the air of the city and not that greasy beer joint, the better off he'd be. He ran home like a certifiable madman, a lunatic, stumbling out of the crumbling brick-veneer building and into the rainy street. He peered nervously around each corner and alleyway he passed, trying to be sure it was safe to venture that way, hoping no addicts or thieves would jump him for his wallet, his coat, his belongings — what if they stole his cellphone, and the recording? Then what? Crossing to the last block, and darting across the street against the red traffic light, an old banged-up Volkswagen Beetle nearly smacked into him, blaring its horn, the driver — an elderly guy with a white crewcut — staring out the window, shaking his fist at Jason and cursing.

Arriving home, he locked the door tight. He stood watching the rain, fingers clamped on his miraculous recording, mind amped up, in a rush of excitement and disbelief. *So this is what it success feels like,* he wondered, and the possibility sent him trembling with elation. *To touch fame and glory. To achieve something extraordinary, the implausible.* The magical fulfillment of every dream he'd ever dared indulge now held in his fingertips.

He hesitated before going to his desk, plugging the cellphone into his laptop, and pressing PLAY on the recording.

What if the recording was blank? No, it *has* to be there, Vincent's voice! Paranoia crept in; he tried to blink the fear away. He took a deep breath, then another, trying to keep his mind straight. Pressing the PLAY button, he stiffened at the click, waiting for the worst. Then Jason listened. *All right, it was there. Every word. Terrific.* He rubbed his hands over his face, staring at the cellphone. He played the entire recording again, then loaded the audio into his laptop, adjusting and balancing the sound levels then quickly pressing SAVE on the file. Hearing van Gogh's voice again chilled him. Sure, it was unbelievable, impossible — *but I saw it, I heard it, I was there! It wasn't just Elena.* He kept trying to rationalize what had happened, to come up with a logical explanation. But did logic even matter? The interview with Vincent was done. He'd spoken with the dead. But was it real? How could he trust it? He didn't believe in ghosts — didn't believe in anything, really. So why did it feel so damn real?

Confident now that the audio file was preserved, Jason recorded his monologue, leveled the master sound track, then logged into his podcast website and carefully uploaded it. When that was done, and the interview with van Gogh was posted — live on the internet — he'd sagged against the table, exhausted.

Now it was hours later, the dead of night. And Jason was unable to sleep. Immense expectations of a bump — no, a life-changing breakthrough — in listener numbers pumped him full of adrenaline. It would fill his desperate and driving need for redemption, connection, healing — for a way to make sense of his pain and to find meaning in his lonely and miserable existence after the death of his child and the collapse of his marriage. Validation! That's what he wanted; to know that his suffering had a purpose, that even a lost soul like himself still had something of value to offer to the world.

At 3:55, Jason closed his eyes, and shook his head, trying to rid it of the sense of purposeless and guilt that consumed his thoughts. The guilt of Judith's death still lingered, after all these years. His mind drifted to the past — his daughter's innocent laughter, his wife's gentle voice. Both were long gone, leaving him adrift. But now, these voices from the other side — Judith's and the voice of van Gogh — filled that silence. They reminded Jason that he wasn't alone. That someone, something, still needed him.

At four o'clock in the morning, he finally fell asleep. The last thing Jason saw before he passed out was a long and winding country road leading into open sunlight — the path to peace.

*   *   *

It was a few minutes before six, and cold, when Jason awoke. He rolled his body out of bed, a dreamy smile on his face. He showered, and shaved for the first time this week. Standing at the sink, his mouth tasted awful; Jason realized with a chuckle that he hadn't brushed his teeth in days. In the kitchen he chugged down two cups of hot coffee. Then he fired up his laptop, and sat at his desk, ready to check the morning numbers on his podcast.

Controlling his nerves, bolstering his confidence, he stretched his shoulders back, and punched in the website address, his eyes brightening as the screen glowed to life. *Probably a good thing if I don't get my expectations too high,* he thought. He spun the numbers in his head. Maybe just a couple of thousand overnight. He leaned forward in his chair, the dreamy smile etched across his face, like a kid on Christmas morning racing to open his gifts from Santa.

His eyes grew moist waiting for the webpage to load. In his mind, he decided that two thousand was a good number, a fair number. An instant later the page snapped to life. And then he saw the current podcast listener numbers for the newest episode of *Echoes.*

Okay, that must be a mistake, Jason thought. He stared at the number until its edges grew soft and blurry. He knew what he was seeing, but it wasn't possible. Was it?

He looked again. Not in the thousands.

Not in the hundreds.

The number was two digits.

12.

Just 12.

The smile on his face crumbled.

For long minutes, Jason stared at the number, waiting, praying for it change. To tick upward. Deflated, he rammed the heels of his hands against his eye sockets, trying to blot out the number. He couldn't make sense of it. Surely this can't be right! He refreshed the page, updating it, waiting, and waiting, watching and staring at the screen with red eyes, the seconds ticking past. He rose from his seat, stalked to the kitchen, fixed another cup of coffee. Refreshing the page and seeing the number stuck at 12 he cocked an eyebrow, nauseated, his brain short-circuiting. What he was seeing wasn't possible; surely he was having delusions.

"Is this a joke?" he said aloud, eyes locked on the screen. Or maybe it wasn't, he thought in horror. Maybe once again, as always, his work was for nothing. All a waste. One impossible dream after another that mocked him.

It seemed as if Jason stood there for years, staring at the laptop screen. At last he walked away, trying not to think about the numbers. Something must be missing, he reasoned. Maybe the internet's down everywhere. He poured the rest of his coffee down the sink, grabbed a beer out of the refrigerator, and took it back to his computer, feeling his fist tighten around the can. He waited ten minutes, then checked the website again. The number hadn't changed. 12. The damn number refused to move! Licking his dry lips, Jason looked at the floor, dumbfounded. Then he slammed the laptop shut, and crushed the can of beer in his fist, foam exploding out.

The air surrounding Jason grew thick as sludge. He oscillated between disbelief and self-doubt. Finally reality set in. He stood, wavering, took a step from the desk, and collapsed to his knees on the mildew-ridden carpet. He began to cry now, in painful, lurching sobs. The tears came hard, his breathing deep. Then he stumbled to the bathroom, and threw up.

Minutes later, he stumbled out, staring around the apartment like he wanted to set it on fire. *Dear God, what happened?* Just an hour before, he had felt such tremendous joy, such incredible hope! No more. Gone. His hopes crushed by the realization that his daydreams were a fraud, that nothing he tried would ever work out, that he'd never accomplish anything great. He felt frightened. *Am I a fool? Am I insane? Insane men deny they're insane. Was it too much to wish? One good thing, one hopeless dream to come true?* For one desperate moment, humiliated beyond anything he'd ever experienced, Jason wanted more than just to run away from his hopeless life, more than to disappear into thin air. He wanted to die.

Death would be final.

Death would be gentle.

Death would be a release.

But no matter how hard he tried, Jason couldn't convince himself, couldn't free his mind trapped in its dizzying cycle of fantasy-reality-fantasy-reality.

Pale, and sick to the bottom of his soul, even here Jason didn't have the courage or the impulse needed to end his life. Finally there was only so much blame he could hang on himself.

Elena. Damn her! he thought. The whisper of her name sent him into a fury. He'd trusted in her, believed in her, placed all his hopes in her. Now he wanted to rush out, find her and grab her by the neck and strangle her.

Without even intending, you've been made a fool of! The sad numbers of van Gogh's *Echoes* podcast put it all into perspective. Maybe the voice really was just Elena! Maybe she was some kind of master manipulator, someone who knew how to read people's misery and pain and give them exactly what they wanted to hear. Jason could rationalize what had happened, coming up with theories about how Elena could have staged the whole supernatural incident at The Silver Spoon, could have conned him into believing he'd heard his dead daughter's voice from the grave, even as a part of Jason wrestled with the feeling that it all was real.

Reinforcing his certainty that Elena was a phony, and had duped him, Jason's skepticism generated wild ideas. When his brain began to clear, he jerked open the laptop, pulled up an internet search engine, and began keywording: *Elena. Medium. Scam. Talk to the dead*, he typed, his fingers hovering over the keys. He needed to know. Was this woman legit? Or was this all a scam?

He searched for her on Google, on Yahoo, on Facebook, wanting to read everything about her, hoping to uncover her criminal past, his eyes scanning the internet with contempt. But there was nothing. *Okay,* he surmised, *let's start over with the facts. Her name is Elena; but what is her surname?* He didn't recall ever hearing it, asking for it — a mistake, on his part. Continuing his hunt for clues, he scanned websites and scrolled down page after page of keyworded results with a merciless intensity, praying to see her face, her photograph. The more chaotic his thoughts became, the more his fingers stabbed at the keyboard. He felt wired, hopped up on burnt coffee, recklessly pressing onward in his obsessed search until his vision was blurry.

An hour later, he'd found nothing. He kept pressing keys, typing in her name, clicking on websites. But it was as if the woman was a blank — *Hell, less than a blank. A nothing!* It was as if she was another ghost; as if Elena didn't exist.

Reaching hysteria, Jason looked at the clock, over by the bed, and then at his cellphone. What is she doing right now? Probably laughing her guts out at him, his ignorance, his childish gullibility. He pictured Elena roaring with laughter as she shared her story in some cocktail bar with the other street con artists. Depression churned in his stomach. Looking at the phone again, it hit him that there was one way he might be able to contact her.

Pulling up her original text message, Jason punched in the number on his phone. To his amazement, on the first ring, Elena answered. Stunned, Jason almost put down the phone and hung up. Was she waiting for him to call?

"Yes, Jason?" she greeted him simply.

Jason's reply was quick, manic, edgy.

"How did you do it? How did you fake those voices? My daughter Judith's? Van Gogh's?" He wanted to choose his words carefully, but his fury rose higher and higher, feeling triumphant in his fiery anger.

There was a hum from the phone line, no reply. At last Elena let out a long sigh. "Is something wrong? You sound tired."

"*Tired?!*" Jason snorted derisively. "I'm pissed-off as hell!" He couldn't believe it. *Incredible! She still expects me to believe it wasn't a con, that it was all real, that she can communicate with the dead!* He began twisting his body around, angry and enraged beyond words. "You lied to me! You said you could speak to the dead!"

"And I was telling the truth. You heard it for yourself."

"So you won't admit it?"

"Admit what?"

"That you've been exploiting my vulnerabilities! My grief! My pain! You pushed and pressed and clawed your way into my already falling-apart, broken-down, screwed-up life, and I believed in you — even though my brain screamed disbelief at your insane claims! Now you've exposed me to public humiliation with this stupid podcast!"

His words must have stunned her, Jason thought, for all he heard was Elena's hushed breath. "Jason, I feel your pain, and I feel your mistrust. Believe me." Hearing this, Jason let out a genuinely surprised laugh. *Can this woman be any more disrespectful? More offensive?* His outrage continued to grow, as Elena spoke again. "You need more evidence. Fine. All I ask is for one final opportunity, one more interview to prove myself."

One more interview?! Jason's mind shrieked. "You must be joking!" His eyes narrowed as he glared at the phone. Her calm voice irritated him now as he stalked and prowled around the room. "Give me one good reason I shouldn't delete the entire van Gogh recording right this second!"

Elena's response came quickly. "Give me one hour. We can meet anywhere you say. Your choice, Jason. I'll be there. And this time," Elena said, "to prove my claims are not fraudulent, that I really can speak with the dead, I will let you select the person we communicate with. I won't know in advance. There will be no way I could prepare my words."

Jason did not reply. Hearing her plan, he flinched. Was this a bluff? In silence he slid his tongue back and forth across his teeth, working to control himself. Then with a startling degree of calm logic taking over his mind, he sat comfortably back in his chair, speaking quietly.

"All right," he said, feeling immediate relief, already thinking of a plan. *What do I have to lose at this point? Another betrayal won't matter. I'm not stupid enough to believe her a second time. And this time I can have the satisfaction of catching her red-handed when she tries to hoodwink me.* "Agreed," he said, as he leaned back and steepled his fingers under his chin. "I'll see you in an hour."

"One hour," Elena repeated. "And this time, Jason," she said, in a tone that chilled Jason right to the bone, "you and the entire world will see and hear the truth."

CHAPTER SIX

The Tears of a Clown

Some wounds echo louder than screams.

An hour later, Jason sat in his kitchen, stress burning a hole in his gut, waiting for Elena to arrive. His fingers tapped a restless rhythm on the edge of his beer can. He didn't know what was coming through that door — a fraud, a hoax, a huckster, a revelation, a resurrection of his dreams...or something far darker than he could ever imagine.

The apartment felt like a pressure cooker, the blue glow of his humming laptop casting restless shadows everywhere, the walls closing in with each passing second. Elena had agreed to meet here this time — The Silver Spoon had served its purpose, she said, and now they needed privacy, a place where they could continue without distractions. *Yes, and a place where my suspicions about you can be exposed,* Jason silently told himself.

He waited, tensely nursing another beer. He could hardly sit still. He told himself he'd stay calm, cool, detached. But already, the plan felt like an unraveling thread in his hands, and Elena was about to pull it loose.

What were the clues he should watch for, the signs that would show she was faking it? Smiling to himself — Elena'd never be prepared for the surprise he had in store — Jason felt genuinely relaxed, calm. Then he heard it: the sharp stiletto click of her heels on the stairwell. His heart stopped. Each step was deliberate, echoing with the inevitability of fate.

Click. Click. Click.

The stabbing sounds on the stairwell cut through the silence like a countdown, each sharp tap echoing the pounding in his chest. Jason swallowed hard, his hands clammy. *She's here.* His brain went into a panic. He mopped the sweat from his face, listening to the sharp footsteps rise, one ominous click at a time…*click!*…*click!*…until he heard the gentle tap-tap-tap on his door.

Jason stood, swaying. Carefully, heart still pounding, he approached the door, unlocked it. It opened an inch. Through the crack he saw the sea-green eyes boring into him.

When the door cracked open, the scent of amber and myrrh drifted in, ancient and intoxicating. Elena stood there, poised, her eyes shimmering like glass over turbulent waters. The wooden box in her hands seemed to hum with its own secret life.

Swallowing his anxiety, Jason smiled at Elena, nodded hello, escorted her inside, then to a chair in the kitchen. As she sat, he opened his laptop, adjusted his recording equipment. Once everything was ready, he planted himself in a chair opposite her, crossing his arms. Instantly his smile changed to a knowing smirk, mocking her, waiting as long as needed for her to ask the question. Not for a second would he let his guard down.

Elena paused, as if playing for time. Jason's heart pounded in his ears. He bit his tongue to keep from saying, *Come on, Elena. Go ahead. Ask me.* Finally, she did.

"Whom shall I contact for our interview?"

Jason's eyes sharpened. Uncrossing his arms, he leaned forward. "Robin Williams," he quipped, staring dead into Elena's face. "I want to speak with Robin Williams. The comedian." Then he sat back in his chair, crossing his arms again defiantly.

Elena scanned Jason's face; they stared each other down. Jason squinted, watching; but her face was unreadable. He waited, drumming his fingers on his left arm. Finally Elena's lips parted, and her voice broke the silence.

"Robin Williams?" she politely asked.

"Yes."

"Now?"

Jason's stomach fluttered. *That's it. Now I've got you,* he thought. "Yes, now." The words snapped out of his lips. "Right now."

Jason hoped to see her panicked reaction, the look of dread on her face; he hoped the words would go through her like a shock. But Elena didn't even raise an eyebrow. Removing her gloves, she carefully placed the carved wooden box on the desktop between them.

"Are you ready, Jason?' she asked, her voice calm, steady, as though she weren't about to summon the voice of a dead man, a man gone too soon, a man she would now guide back from the grave.

She's going through all the motions! Jason thought to himself. *No kidding, she's going to pull out all the stops to try and fool me!* his mind chuckled, thinking it was incredibly silly. Skeptically he studied Elena; she seemed lost in thought, her back curved forward, head tilted, her eyes closed as she prepared herself.

This time, she'd need to fake the idiosyncratic voice of Robin Williams, a legendary comic whose off-the-wall humor had brought joy to millions, even as he silently battled his own demons. Robin Williams was a figure Jason had always admired, whose voice in movies and TV and stand-up comedy routines he knew intimately. It was for that reason, he smiled to himself, that Jason had chosen the comedian.

The wooden box sat between them, its surface etched with intricate and mysterious patterns Jason couldn't decipher. It looked ancient, weighty, as if it held not just secrets but consequences.

"I'm ready. Are you?" Jason asked.

Elena opened her eyes slowly and nodded. "Yes. Robin is eager to speak. But be prepared, Jason. This one... this one is different. He carries a heavy burden, one that laughter could never truly lift."

Jason swallowed hard, his throat dry. He wasn't sure if he was ready, but there was no turning back now. Remaining skeptical — *We'll see if this woman is a fake or not now* — he pressed RECORD on his cellphone, sliding it closer to Elena. He nodded for her to begin, and she closed her eyes once more, her breathing steady and deep.

Around them the apartment grew colder, then icy — a biting cold that seeped into your bones and whispered of places where warmth had never existed — the air thickening then swirling. The cold clawed at Jason's skin, and made his chest ache. He shivered, hugging himself; for a moment, he swore he saw the faintest trace of a mist escape Elene's lips as she exhaled. Behind them the refrigerator let out a stuttering hum, then fell silent. Jason watched, as Elena's face began to change. It softened, unexplainably looking younger, her expression shifting into something more relaxed, looser, freer, and more...*What?* Jason struggled to put his finger on it. *Familiar. That's what it was.* Her mouth curled into a mischievous grin. When she spoke, the voice no longer belonged to Elena — it was a voice that drove Jason back into his chair in shock. It wasn't just the legendary Robin Williams — it was every room he'd every lit up, every heart he'd ever touched, speaking through her. Once again, he was in the presence of the dead.

"Hellooo, Jason!" the voice burst out, playful and unmistakable. Jason froze. It was him. Robin Williams. His voice danced through the room, brimming with life and energy. "So, this is the big moment, huh? Gotta say, I wasn't expecting to show up at a kitchen table. No red carpet? Not even a fruit platter? Man, the afterlife budget is tighter than I thought!" From Elena's throat came an unmistakable chuckle. "It's good to be here, though I gotta say, folks, it's a little colder than I expected!" the comedian quipped, then paused for the punchline. "Whoa, Jason, helluva setup you've got here. What's the theme? Post-apocalyptic chic? Or is this your audition for an episode of *Hoarders*?"

Jason couldn't help but smile, despite the tension in his chest. *How is she doing this? She had no idea, no clue what person I'd select for her to speak with!* Yet here the unmistakable voice of Robin Williams was! Startled, Jason quickly replied, "Robin, I've been a fan of yours for as long as I can remember."

"Oh, stop it, you're making me blush! Or, well, I would be if I still had blood in my veins!" Robin bantered, the dark humor in his voice unmistakable. "Speaking of which, being dead isn't all bad, you know. No taxes, no spam emails. But the Wi-Fi? Abysmal! Somebody call Steve Jobs — we need an upgrade!"

Jason burst out laughing. When he suddenly stopped, trying his best to hide his chuckles, he could no longer resist or ignore the truth: impossible or not, he really *was* talking to the real Robin Williams.

"But seriously, folks," Robin interrupted, "while it's nice to be remembered, even after all this time, let's get this show on the road! Where would you like to start?"

For a moment, Jason neither moved nor replied, still in shock. Earnestly he stared at Elena, troubled by his unfounded suspicions, his hunch that she was a fake. Then Jason took a deep breath, trying to stay focused. Where to start? He'd neglected to write down any questions, certain his premonitions about Elena were correct. Quickly he brooded. "Robin, the world knew you as one of the funniest people alive. You brought so much joy to so many. But… I think a lot of people also sensed that there was something more, something darker beneath the surface. Can you tell us about that?"

When Robin spoke again, his voice had lost some of its playfulness. "Ah, yes. The ol' tears of a clown routine. The thing about us funny folks, Jason, is that our tears aren't ours. We're the reservoirs for everyone else's pain. When you laugh, we cry a little less. But sometimes, even the biggest laugh in the world can't fill the well." Robin paused. "It's funny, isn't it? Okay, maybe it's *not* so funny when you're the one tagged by the whole world as a comedic genius. Whole lotta pressure to perform comes with that gig. Like with my friend John Belushi — the poor guy struggled with drugs and personal demons throughout his life. Pretty freakin' weird how the ones who make others laugh the hardest are often the ones crying the most on the inside, dontcha think?

"'But let me tell you something about being here, Jason. You don't bring your Oscars, your standing ovations, or even your funniest jokes. You only bring the moments that mattered — the ones where you showed up, even if your heart was breaking."

Jason nodded. He'd heard stories about other comics, like Belushi, Andy Kaufman and Richard Pryor, haunted by their never-ending battles with alcohol and drugs, particularly cocaine and angel dust, and their bouts with anxiety and fear and depression. Trying to numb their hidden trauma with painkillers.

"You know what comedy really is, Jason? It's armor. Every joke I cracked was another link in the chainmail I wrapped around my soul. But even armor has cracks, and sometimes the torment and the darkness slips through.'"

Jason felt an icy chill in the air that made his pulse quicken. He knew that the conversation with Robin was about to go deeper, touching on truths that would resonate far beyond the confines of this interview.

"Robin," Jason began, his voice steadying as he prepared to dive into the complexities of the man before him, "I seem to recall you once said, 'I think the saddest people always try their hardest to make people happy. Because they know what it feels like to feel absolutely worthless and they don't want anybody else to feel like that.' Can you tell me more about what you meant? Despite all of your fame, why did you feel worthless?"

"You know, Jason," Robin replied, his voice suddenly quieter, tinged with the weight of lived experience, "people often see the laughter, the smiles, the jokes, but they rarely see the struggle that lies beneath. The jokes hide a frightened human being. Humor was my shield, my way of deflecting the darkness, not just for myself but for others too. I knew what it felt like to be at the bottom, to feel like nothing you do matters. And the last thing I wanted was for anyone else to feel that way. That part came from trying to please my mother — I was always trying to be funny for her, accepted by her. My first audience was my Mom. I made her laugh to fill the silence, the awful void, to feel like I mattered. Funny thing is, I never stopped performing for her, even when she wasn't there. That was my never-ending struggle — before the drugs. But when I saw even a beast like my friend Belushi couldn't handle the drugs, that sobered the shit out of me. So, I did what I did best:

I made people laugh. I made them feel good. I made them happy, because if they were happy, then maybe, just maybe, I could keep the sadness at bay, for them and for myself. Even if just for one moment…

"But life isn't about chasing happiness, Jason. It's about making meaning. And the beautiful, painful truth is, the two don't always overlap.'"

Jason nodded, absorbing Robin's words, feeling the deep empathy and compassion that had driven him. "That must have been exhausting, though. To carry that enormous pressure."

"Trust me. It was," Robin admitted, his voice carrying the echoes of that burden. "But it was also necessary. Just part of the comic's calling. It's a strange thing, being driven by the fear of worthlessness. It makes you push harder, give more, try like hell to be funnier, because you can't stand the thought of someone else suffering like you have. But it's a double-edged sword, Jason. Seriously, I talk about this all the time with my best buddy Jonathan Winters, the wild man. He's up here somewhere in Comedy Heaven. Because while you're busy making everyone else feel better, you're slowly chipping away at yourself."

Jason's thoughts swirled, trying to comprehend the vast emotional landscape that Robin navigated throughout his life. He thought of another quote, one that had always stuck with him, and decided to ask. "You once said, 'You're only given a little spark of madness. You mustn't lose it.' Can you talk about that spark, that madness, and what it meant to you?"

A soft chuckle filled the air, tinged with a hint of nostalgia. "Ah, the spark, the madness, the insanity!" Robin mused. "Madness, Jason, is the world's way of telling you, 'Hey, you're still alive.' Don't snuff it out. Feed it, protect it, let it burn bright. Because when the madness is gone, so is the magic. That's the thing that kept me going, Jason. That little bit of madness, that touch of the absurd, the obsession with being funny no matter what it cost…it's what fueled my creativity. Seriously: come inside my brain and take a look!" Robin wisecracked, and Jason chuckled. "It's what made the world make sense in a way that nothing else could. The spark of psycho-insane riffing on whatever popped into my head — that was my gift, my curse, and my salvation all rolled into one. It's what allowed me to see the world differently, to turn pain into laughter, to make the mundane magical. But the thing about that spark is, you have to protect it. The world has a way of trying to snuff it out, trying to make you conform, to fit into neat little boxes. And once you lose it, you lose a part of yourself."

Jason could hear the passion in Robin's voice, the deep connection he had to his own unique brand of creativity. "Did you ever feel like you were losing it? That the world was closing in?"

"Hell yes," Robin confessed, his tone now more somber. "There were times when the spark flickered, when I felt like I was drowning in pressure, in anxiety, in expectations — my own, the world's. But I held on, Jason. I held on because that spark was all I had. It was the only thing that made me feel alive, that made me feel like I had something worth giving."

Jason leaned back, digesting the depth of Robin's insights. He then decided to bring up another one of Robin's famous quotes, one that seemed particularly poignant given the nature of their conversation. "Another thing you said is this: 'I used to think the worst thing in life was to end up all alone. It's not. The worst thing in life is to end up with people who make you feel all alone.' What led you to that realization?"

A heavy sigh echoed through the kitchen. "Loneliness isn't about being alone, Jason. It's about being surrounded by people who don't understand you, who don't see you. I was often in rooms full of people, surrounded by celebrities and fans and groupies and laughter and applause, but still felt isolated. It's a terrible thing, to be in a crowd and feel like you're invisible. I learned the hard way that it's better to be truly alone than to be with people who make you feel that way. It's not the absence of people, Jason, that makes you feel lonely. It's being unseen, unheard, even when the whole world is watching. The spotlight doesn't warm you when you're standing in the dark.'"

The vulnerability in Robin's voice resonated with Jason, striking a chord deep within him. "That must have been incredibly painful," he said, his own heart aching at the thought.

"It was," Robin replied softly. "But it also taught me the value of genuine connection. It made me cherish those rare moments when I felt truly seen, truly understood. That's what we all want, Jason. To be seen, to be understood, to know that we matter to someone."

Jason swallowed hard, the emotion of the moment nearly overwhelming him. "Robin, I'm sure many of our listeners will resonate with what you're saying. You also once said, 'Comedy is acting out optimism.' Was that your way of coping with the pain?"

"Yes," Robin responded, the warmth returning to his voice. "Comedy was my way of saying that no matter how dark things got, there was always a glimmer of hope. Hope was my way of fighting back against the shadows. Laughter is powerful, Jason. It's a way of reclaiming joy, of saying that the darkness doesn't win. That's why I kept going, why I kept making people laugh. Because if I could make someone smile, even for a moment, then maybe the world wasn't such a bad place after all."

Jason felt a deep sense of gratitude for Robin's honesty, for the way he laid bare the truth of his life and struggles. "You also believed in the power of words, didn't you? I remember you said, 'No matter what people tell you, words and ideas can change the world.' Did you always feel that way?"

"I did," Robin affirmed. "Words are powerful. They can uplift, inspire, tear down, or heal. My whole life was about using words to make people think, to make them feel, to make them laugh. I believed that if you could reach someone with a word, with an idea, you could change the course of their life. It's why I never took my work lightly. I knew that every word I spoke had the potential to impact someone, somewhere."

Jason was moved by the conviction in Robin's voice. "It's clear that you cared deeply about your work, about the impact you had on others. But you also understood the importance of being authentic, didn't you? You once said, 'For a while, you get mad, then you get over it.' How did that philosophy guide you?"

Robin's laughter filled the room, an impish sound that was both light and laden with meaning. "Life is full of frustrations, Jason. I remember staying up late with my Dad, watching *The Tonight Show With Johnny Carson*, sneaking peeks at my Dad, waiting to see him laugh. He was a sweet guy, but he never laughed. There were plenty of times when I got mad, when things didn't go the way I wanted, when I felt like the world was against me. But you can't stay mad forever. It eats you up inside. You have to let it go, to move on, to find the humor in it all. That's what kept me going — the ability to laugh at myself, at the absurdity of life, to find a way through the madness."

Jason couldn't help but smile at Robin's resilience, at the way he found strength in humor. "You also had some interesting thoughts on love and relationships. You once said, 'I think the idea of there being a true soulmate for everybody is the absolute biggest myth on earth. But that's what people search for, which is why they end up unhappy when they can't find that one person.' What did you mean?"

Robin's voice took on a more introspective tone. "People have this idea that there's one perfect person out there for them, and if they don't find that person, then they're doomed to be unhappy. But that's not how it works. Love is about connection, about finding someone who understands you, who sees you for who you really are. It's not about perfection. It's about being with someone who makes the journey of life a little bit easier, a little bit brighter, the path ahead smoother. Waiting for a perfect soulmate can make you miss out on the real, imperfect connections that are right in front of you."

Jason felt his eyes watering. Their exchange had become deeply personal, and cathartic, challenging his unresolved grief and guilt. His voice trembled as he asked the question that had haunted him for years.

"Did you ever feel like…like you couldn't do enough? That you'd let someone down?"

Immediately Robin's voice lost its playful edge. "Every damn day, kid. But here's the thing: you can't save everyone. Sometimes, the best you can do is show up, give it all you've got, and forgive yourself for the rest."

Jason swallowed hard, his vision blurring. "But what if you *can't* forgive yourself?"

Robin's reply came gently, like a hushed breath through the icy air. "Then you keep trying. Because forgiveness isn't a finish line, Jason. It's a path you walk every day."

Jason let those words sink in, feeling the hard truth. Eyes half closed, he thought of his wife Sarah, his daughter Judith, feeling the enormous hole left by their loss. Would he forever be grieving this? He knew that this conversation with Robin was one that would stay with him, one that would resonate with his listeners in ways he couldn't yet fully grasp. "Robin, you've shared so much with us today. Your words will no doubt touch the hearts of many. Is there anything else you'd like to say? Any final thoughts?"

Robin's voice, filled with a mix of warmth and gravitas, replied, "Just remember, Jason, that life is messy, complicated, chaotic, and sometimes downright painful. But it's also beautiful, filled with moments of joy, connection, and love. Don't take any of it for granted. What everyone really wants is to know that they're not alone in the madness. That their spark, their fire, means something. Life's messy...it's messy and screwed-up as hell. It's joy and sorrow, madness and magic, all rolled into one. We can't avoid the mess — but we can embrace it. Embrace the madness, the insanity, the laughter, the tears. The freedom to do crazy shit, to just be *alive*. And most of all, be kind — to others, and to yourself. Because in the end, that's all that really matters. And never forget the words of my *Dead Poets Society* character, Professor Keating: 'Carpe diem.'"

The voice faded, signifying the end of the interview. The room seemed to settle, the cold chill subsiding, a quiet peace descending as Jason absorbed Robin's final words. He sat back in his seat, his mind drifting off. His eyes were wet, he realized. He felt a profound sense of connection, not just to Robin, but to the vast tapestry of life itself. This conversation had been more than an interview; it had been a journey into the heart of what it means to be human.

As the energy in the air warmed and shifted back to normal, Elena composed herself at the kitchen table. Jason stared at the carved wooden box, its patterns swirling in the dim light like a secret just out of reach. For the first time in years, he didn't feel lost. He felt...*seen.* Then before he could say anything Elena slipped the mysterious carved box back into her handbag, slid on her gloves, rose confidently from her chair. And without a word she left the apartment.

Sitting alone in the kitchen, Jason shivered. He stared at his cellphone, still recording, until his head ached. Then he pressed the STOP RECORDING and SAVE buttons, stood and clicked off the lights in the kitchen. He walked around the apartment, his mind now a blank, then shuffled and bumped his way into the bathroom. Jason knew that this episode of *Echoes* would be one that people would talk about for years to come. It was an episode that, like Robin Williams himself, would leave an indelible mark on all who listened.

Returning to the kitchen for his cellphone, Jason hovered over it a moment, trembling. He pressed the PLAY button, his breath catching, expecting to hear Robin's laughter again. Instead, there was only static. The static hissed like a live wire. A second later came the voice, crackling but clear: "Jason…it's Robin. Hey, buddy. Seize the day." He dropped the phone, his pulse racing. Robin hadn't said those words during the recording. And yet, there they were!

Jason darted to the kitchen sink, and splashed cold water on his face. *Do you need any more evidence?* he asked himself. *No,* he decided with a heavy sigh. All the evidence, all the truth he needed was now preserved on more than his cellphone; it was carved deep on his heart. Now he was convinced. He'd begun the day cynical and lost, but ended it with proof that Elena's gift of channeling the dead was real — albeit shaken, questioning everything he knew about life, death, and purpose. Now Jason believed, beyond a shadow of a doubt. But would the world also believe?

CHAPTER SEVEN

The Restless Wandering Spirit

Restless spirits wander paths paved with regret.

Jason's hands trembled as he poured coffee, the steaming liquid sloshing over the rim of the mug, the mug rattling on the counter like a warning bell. *Calm down,* he told himself, as he juggled and balanced the hot drink across the room to his laptop. He couldn't tell if it was the caffeine, the sleepless nights, or the thought of what lay ahead — the next interview with the dead, a voice reaching across the void. He prayed his podcast was growing, but there was the gnawing sense that he was playing with forces he barely understood.

Powering up his computer, Jason clicked on his web browser, and waited. He felt a sudden urgency to check the number of listeners from the Robin Williams podcast.

In dread he watched the page glow to life, the statistics loading, fearing that all his work was in vain and that he was destined to be an underachieving failure. As the numbers appeared Jason suddenly gasped and grabbed the laptop with both hands. It took a few groggy seconds for him to realize what he was seeing.

412 downloads! Jason nearly choked on scalding coffee when he saw the number. Not only were the listener statistics creeping up, but now his second *Echoes* podcast was being shared — and there were eleven comments posted from excited listeners.

An exhilarating feeling pounded in Jason's brain. He tried to look away from the numbers, but could not. He waited fifteen minutes, refreshed the podcast page, and saw the download numbers continue to creep higher, taking a jump to 417, then 418.

This is fantastic! Jason thought. *Curiosity is driving word-of-mouth!* Jason's fingers throbbed as he feverishly typed and scanned the site analytics. Perhaps the boost had come from his handful of hardcore listeners; perhaps newfound fans were obsessively sharing the Robin Williams episode — whatever had happened, this growth would surely skyrocket as Jason continued to release more and more interviews with other famous members of the dead.

For 30 minutes, Jason sat at his computer, refreshing the podcast stats, reading the responses, studying the statistics. Then he sat back from the laptop, and rubbed his weary eyes.

"557 downloads," he said aloud, tasting the words in his mouth. The number sparked an explosion of glee in his mind, his body buzzing. He tilted his head and daydreamed — and as he did, as his brain exploded in gleeful triumph, the desperation for *Echoes* to transform his life and rid it forevermore of its emptiness, its unworthiness, its loneliness reappeared, and the craving need to redeem all of Jason's losses returned.

557 downloads, he sighed. A number too small to satisfy but too large to ignore. The success tasted bittersweet, like a meal he couldn't quite finish. The hunger for more downloads gnawed at him, sharper than any hunger for food or fame.

557 isn't enough, he admitted to himself. The overnight growth in listeners wasn't bad; but Jason himself was still a nobody, an anonymous struggling podcaster, and *Echoes* a cipher, a trivial nonentity. Real success was not going to happen unless he could convince a larger audience that he was really speaking with the dead, offering a voyeuristic tour of the afterlife.

Besides, it's not just about numbers, Jason told himself. It was about proving something — to himself, to the world. That he could matter. That he wasn't just a restless wandering spirit, chasing shadows in the dark.

He needed to come up with a strategy to increase the listener numbers. But how? His mind groped. There was nothing anywhere on the internet — hell, in the entire history of the planet — like *Echoes*. A man who can speak with the dead! Sensational! Yet still it was struggling. How to grab the ears and minds of listeners in a world of constant chaos and shrinking attention spans?

For hours, Jason sat, in deep concentration, gazing into space, working on his plan of attack. He had bigger goals than a few hundred downloads, a smattering of comments. The obvious challenge was immense: getting the online community to flood the internet with his podcasts. To realize this vision, *Echoes* needed to go viral. Become a *cause célèbre*. Produce material that was not just astonishing, not just mind-boggling, but shocking, controversial, disturbing —

Nothing could stop this quest. Yet there were only two days left until the next interview. What to do?

* * *

"Jason, are you ready?"

Jason's heart thudded in his ears. He stood at the window of his shabby apartment, illuminated by the blinding noonday sun, the roar of the city outside — honking cars and speeding trucks and booming airplanes — rumbling through the air. On the kitchen table the empty file for the next podcast recording was loading onto his laptop screen. Minutes before, he'd ushered Elena into the building. Now Elena sat in a kitchen chair, digging into her handbag, calling his name.

"Jason?"

Jason rubbed his sweaty palms, his body swirling in pure adrenaline. For two days, the echoes of his previous interviews reverberated in his mind, leaving him emotionally exhausted yet paradoxically driven. Each conversation had chipped away at his defenses, uncovering a raw desire to dig deeper, to unearth the hidden truths of those who had lived extraordinary lives. Today, he was about to engage with Anthony Bourdain — celebrity chef, best-selling author, and renowned travel documentarian. A man who had inspired millions, yet whose life was marked by a relentless, all-consuming search for meaning. And a man whose life ended tragically, by his own hand.

The way it ended was what intrigued Jason. Excited him. Pumped him full of euphoria — until the only fear he had was being able to contain the anxiety he felt about his secret plan.

The past few days had been a whirlwind of immersion into Bourdain's world. Jason had devoured the man's writings, his best-selling books, his voice on every page tenacious and gritty and unfiltered. He watched episode after episode of *Parts Unknown*, Bourdain's hit TV show, exploring cultures and cuisines all across the globe, feeling the pulse of the places Bourdain had traveled to, the rawness of the human experience laid bare. Bourdain wasn't just a celebrity or a chef; he was a poet of the unglamorous, a ribald storyteller who found beauty in the dark and twisted corners of the globe. And because of this, Jason knew this conversation would be unlike any other, and would radically change the future for *Echoes*.

"Jason? I asked if you're ready."

Elena's voice snapped Jason out of his reverie, back to reality. He looked up, startled. It was time for the interview. Taking his seat in the kitchen, he hunched over his microphone, the laptop ready and humming,

Elena's hands trembled as she removed the wooden conduit box from her bag. Jason noticed the shadows under her eyes, the weariness that clung to her like a second skin. "Ready?" she asked again, her voice calm but strained, as though she were preparing to wrestle the dead into submission.

Jason gulped. "Yes. I'm ready."

As he said this, and Elena closed her eyes and focused, the air surrounding them thickened, the temperature dipping and dropping like a sudden winter storm. An icelike throbbing knifed through Jason's stomach. His breath hung in front of him, his heartbeat pounding louder than the city's noise outside. He watched Elena's closed eyelids flutter. He watched her chin shudder, the skin seeming to stretch tight across her cheeks, her body rocking back and forth, her features shifting into a contemplative state that eerily mirrored the man they were about to commune with. Then the voice came, gravelly and alive, cutting through the silence. The voice was unmistakably Anthony Bourdain's — gravelly, introspective, and tinged with weariness.

"Hey, Jason," Tony's voice carried the easy cadence of an old friend. "So this is what it feels like on the other side, huh? Not bad."

A smile tugged at Jason's lips, the tension in his shoulders easing just a bit. "Mr. Bourdain…Tony…it's an honor. Thank you for being here."

"Yeah, well, 'here' is a relative term, isn't it?" Tony's voice was edged with the familiar sardonic, wry humor that had endeared him to so many. "I've eaten blowfish and drunk moonshine with strangers in the jungle, but talking to you from beyond the grave? This is a first. But let's not get bogged down in details. We've got ground to cover."

Jason nodded, bracing himself for the conversation ahead. "Tony, your work — your writing, your TV shows — had such a profound impact on people. You showed the world in a way that was raw, real, and unfiltered. But I know that perspective came from a place of deep struggle. What drove you to keep pushing, to keep exploring, even when it must have been so exhausting?"

"What drove me?" Bourdain asked. "Hell, I don't know. Maybe it was the fear of standing still. I was always running, always searching for something…anything to fill the void. That's the thing about restlessness — it keeps you moving, your spirit forever wandering, but it never lets you find peace. I was always chasing the next meal, the next story, the next thrill, hoping it would be the one to finally make me feel whole. But it never was…

"Restlessness isn't just a habit, Jason," Bourdain continued. "It's a disease. Restlessness is a fire. It can light the way, but if you're not careful, it'll burn everything down. It's a hunger that doesn't quit, that gnaws at your gut even when you're full. It's what drove me to the ends of the earth, but it's also what made me feel like I never had a home."

Jason nodded, pursing his lips. *When should I start executing my plan?* he pondered. He waffled, struggling to make up his mind. Nervously he decided to lead slowly into the question he planned to ask Bourdain. Meanwhile, he would bide his time.

"Did you ever find satisfaction in the journey, in the places you visited, the people you met?" he asked.

Bourdain let out a small, rueful laugh. "Satisfaction? Sure, in bits and pieces. There were moments — fleeting, beautiful moments — when I felt connected, like I was part of something bigger than myself. But those moments never lasted. I'd be onto the next thing before I could even appreciate what I'd just experienced. It was like I was trying to outrun my own mind, always needing to be somewhere else, doing something else, because if I stopped…well, I didn't want to think about what would happen if I stopped."

The exhaustion in Tony's voice was palpable, the weariness of a man who had lived a thousand lives yet never found a true home in any of them. Jason shifted in his seat, the heaviness of the conversation pressing down on him. "You once said that 'Travel isn't always pretty. It isn't always comfortable. Sometimes it hurts, it even breaks your heart. But that's okay. The journey changes you; it *should* change you. It leaves marks on your memory, on your consciousness, on your heart, and on your body. You take something with you. Hopefully, you leave something good behind.' How did the journey change you, Tony?"

Tony's voice was filled with wistful reflection. "It changed me in ways I never expected. It opened my eyes to the world, to the beauty and the ugliness, to the kindness and the cruelty. It made me see things I could never unsee, feel things I could never forget. And it made me realize just how small I was in the grand scheme of things. But it also made me appreciate the moments of connection, the times when I felt truly alive. Those moments were rare, but they were worth all the pain, all the heartache…

"The thing about travel, Jason," Bourdain continued, his tone weary, "is it strips you down to your bones. You see the world for what it really is — beautiful, messy, tragic, and sublime. It leaves you raw, but it also makes you feel alive in a way nothing else can."

Jason paused, growing more nervous. Getting to the question was taking forever. He felt like pushing Bourdain; instead he leaned forward, and spoke into the microphone. "Tony, your travels weren't just about seeing new places — they were about connecting with people, with cultures. You said, 'You learn a lot about someone when you share a meal together.' How did food play into that connection?"

Tony chuckled. "Food was everything, Jason. It was the ultimate connector. You can sit down with someone from the other side of the world, who doesn't speak your language, doesn't share your beliefs, but over a meal, you can find common ground. Food breaks down barriers, it opens doors. It's a way of saying, 'I'm here, I want to understand you.' And in those moments, when you're sharing a meal, you're not just eating — you're participating in something ancient, something primal, something universal, and deeply human. In those moments, you're living, my friend. Really living."

Jason nodded, the simplicity of Tony's words resonating. He distracted himself from his nervous mind by drumming his fingers on his lap. *Calm down,* he scolded himself. *You need to stay calm! Don't be hasty! The right moment will come.* "But beyond food, there was something else in your travels — an honesty, an authenticity that shone through. You never shied away from showing the rough edges of the world. You said, 'I don't have to agree with you to like you or respect you.' How did that belief shape your experiences?"

Tony's voice took on a more serious tone. "It's easy to judge, to look at someone's life and say, 'I wouldn't do it that way,' or 'I don't agree with that.' But the truth is, we're all just trying to make our way through this world the best we can. I've met people who lived in ways I couldn't understand, who believed things I couldn't relate to, but that didn't mean I couldn't respect them, couldn't find value in their perspective. That's what travel does — it forces you to confront the reality that your way isn't the only way. And once you accept that, the world opens up to you in ways you never imagined."

Jason could feel the truth in Tony's words, the wisdom that had come from a life lived on the edge, always pushing boundaries. "You were known for taking risks, for embracing uncertainty. You once urged people, especially the young, to 'travel — as far and as widely as possible. Sleep on floors, if you have to. Find out how other people live, eat, and cook. Learn from them — wherever you go.' What made you so passionate about that?"

Tony's voice lightened, as if recalling the joy of his younger days. "Because that's how you *grow*, Jason. That's how you become more than what you were born into. There's a whole world out there, full of experiences and lessons that you can't get from a book or a TV show or a classroom. You have to get out there, see it for yourself, taste it, live it! It's not always going to be easy, but that's the point. Growth doesn't happen in comfort zones — it happens when you're uncomfortable, pushed to your limits, when you're forced to confront the unknown."

Jason couldn't help but admire Bourdain's relentless pursuit of life, even when it led him down dark and difficult paths. As Tony spoke, Jason felt himself sinking deeper into the man's words, the honesty in his voice both inspiring and unsettling. It was as if Bourdain's restlessness mirrored his own — the unrelenting need to prove himself, to matter. Jason wondered if he was running, too, chasing something he couldn't name.

"But that kind of life," Jason said, "it must have taken its toll. You were open about your struggles, about the reality of suffering. You once said, 'I understand there's a guy inside me who wants to lay in bed, smoke weed all day, and watch cartoons and old movies. My whole life is a series of stratagems to avoid and outwit that guy.' How did you manage to keep moving forward despite those challenges?"

Tony's response was tinged with a bittersweet understanding. "I didn't always manage. There were days when the darkness won, when that guy inside me got the better of me. But I kept going because I had to. There were stories to tell, people to meet, meals to share. And I guess, in some way, those things kept me alive — they gave me a reason to get out of bed, to keep fighting. But it wasn't easy. And it wasn't always enough."

The heaviness of the conversation settled over Jason, squeezing at his heart, picking at his brain. Still there was more to explore. "You also talked a lot about cultural respect, about approaching other ways of life with humility. You said, 'To be treated well in places where you don't expect to be treated well, to find things in common with people you've never met, to make unlikely friends — that's one of the great things about travel.' How did that respect shape your interactions?"

Tony's voice grew thoughtful, reflective. "It's about recognizing that the world doesn't revolve around you, Jason. When you travel, you're a guest in someone else's home, someone else's culture. You have to approach that with respect, with an open mind. You're there to learn, not to impose your own values or beliefs. And when you do that — when you really listen, when you show that you're there to understand — you find connections in the most unexpected places. You make friends where you thought you'd find enemies. It's one of the most beautiful things about travel, and about life."

Nervously listening, Jason sat hunched over his microphone, looking down at his list of questions, his brain thick with waiting. *Now? Yes, now. No more of this damn waiting. Ask the question.*

"Tony, let's talk about your death…your suicide. What was that moment like?"

Immediately there was silence. Jason waited, staring into space. He wiped his hand anxiously across his chin. As the silence grew longer, panic began to settle in. At last he saw Elena's lips move, and there was a note of sarcastic outrage in the voice from beyond.

"You mean the moment I hung myself in my bathroom? That moment?"

Jason snapped upright in his chair, eyes open, blinking. The words stunned him. *Oh God. Oh no. Now what?* His body went suddenly numb. For terror-filled seconds he didn't know what to say. His hand reached for the STOP RECORDING button — but it was too late.

"You want to know what it felt like, Jason? All right, I'll tell you. It felt like slipping out of a suit that never fit right. Peaceful, at first. But the thing they don't tell you is, the pain doesn't end. It just transfers to the people you leave behind. And that's a weight I wouldn't wish on anyone…

"Listen," Bourdain said, "I'm not proud of what I did. Do I regret it? Taking my own life? Yeah. Not for me, but for them — the people I loved, who have to carry my absence like a scar that never heals. You see, I had the best job in the world. The greatest job! Yet I always felt like a freak, like Quasimodo, the Hunchback of Notre Dame, isolated in my tower, tormented in my loneliness. I would find myself in an airport, ordering a hamburger. Suddenly I'd look at the hamburger and find myself in a spiral of depression that would last for days…

"'That's not so bad,' I'd tell myself. 'It's alright. I'll make it.' I'd have a couple of happy minutes where I'd think life is pretty damn good. But I was forever battling depression, and never reaching out for help, never asking somebody to save me."

Jason leaned back in his chair, staring at Elena. He felt as if he were seeing the real Anthony Bourdain through her, the air shimmering, blurred, ghostly, Bourdain's words crashing through his brain, then blown out into the light.

"I was a perfectionist," Bourdain continued, "and left no time for my loved ones when the shooting was finished. I pushed myself — *hard*. I should have died in my twenties — but I was just too neurotic, driven. I deluded myself into thinking I'd be happy if I pushed myself harder. So what did the moment of death feel like? Peace. Tranquility. I went to death fearlessly. My pain was over. I *wanted* to die…

"What I never thought about," Bourdain stated, his voice strained now, sounding fragile, "was those I'd leave behind. My loved ones are forever traumatized, tortured by a pain that can never subside. What I did to them is unforgivable. They're the ones who have suffered, not me. My suffering is over. Theirs is eternal."

Hearing this, Jason's mouth went suddenly dry. Tears welled up behind his eyelids. He could see how these frailties and failures had propelled Tony to end his life — yet had also driven and motivated Bourdain to survive through every intensely-chaotic stage of his journey. Unexpectedly, Jason felt compassion — and as the tears sprang out, he silently rubbed them away.

"Tony, thank you for answering that. You found joy in the simple pleasures of life — good food, good company, the beauty of everyday experiences. You once said, 'Your body is not a temple, it's an amusement park. Enjoy the ride.' How did that philosophy influence the way you lived?"

Tony chuckled, a sound that seemed to carry both joy and resignation. "Life is too short, dammit, to deny yourself the things that make you happy. We spend so much time worrying about what we should do, what we're supposed to do, that we forget to actually *live*. For me, the simple pleasures — sitting down to a good meal, sharing a laugh with friends, experiencing the beauty of a sunset — those were the things that made life worth living. They didn't solve my problems, but they made the journey a little easier, a little more enjoyable…

"'Life isn't a straight line. It's a patchwork of moments — some beautiful, some brutal. The trick isn't to hold onto them. It's to let them shape you and keep you moving. Even when it feels like the world is too heavy, there's light somewhere. You just have to look for it. And if you can't find it, create it.'"

Jason felt a deep connection to Tony in that moment, a shared understanding of the struggles they both faced. "You're right, life is fleeting, isn't it?" he said. "You often reflected on the impermanence of life, saying, 'We are, after all, temporary arrangements of molecules as much as we are meat, bone, and blood. Every day we wake up is another chance to get it right.' How did that awareness shape your choices?"

Tony's voice softened. "It made me appreciate the moments. It made me realize that nothing is guaranteed, that every day is a gift. And it pushed me to live fully, to embrace the chaos and the beauty of life. I wasn't always successful, but

I tried. And that's all any of us can do — try our damndest to get it right, even if just for a moment…

"We're all just wandering spirits, Jason. Trying to find a home in a world that was never meant to be permanent."

Jason wiped at his eyes, his heart aching for the man who had given so much to the world, only to feel so lost. "Tony… I'm so sorry. I'm sorry that you felt like you had to carry that burden alone."

"Don't be sorry, Jason," Tony replied gently. "It's part of the human condition, isn't it? We all have our burdens, our battles to fight. Mine just happened to be a little more visible than most. But if there's one thing I've learned, it's that we don't have to fight them alone. We can reach out; we can ask for help. And that's not a sign of weakness — it's a sign of strength."

Jason began his final question softly. "Tony, what message would you give to listeners who might be going through a rough patch in their lives? What would you say to them?"

Bourdain laughed. "Advice about life? From me? A man who desperately needed help, but refused to ask for it? Who hung himself?" Jason blinked; he sat back in his chair, shocked that Bourdain could speak so matter-of-factly. "Life is complicated, Jason. It's chaotic, it's shitty, and sometimes it can feel like the ugliness and the chaos of the world is too much to bear. But I want them to know that they are not alone in their struggles. There is always someone who cares, who will listen, who will help them find their way back to the light. They don't have to carry the burden by themselves."

Tony's voice sounded tender now, a note of finality creeping in. "It's okay to ask for help, that it doesn't make any of us weak or a failure. It makes us *human.* We are all human, Jason, and we all need each other to get through this life. Sometimes the bravest thing you can do is to reach out and say, 'I'm struggling; I need help.' And that's okay. It's more than okay — it's necessary."

Jason let it all sink in. Then Bourdain said, almost pleadingly, "Thank you, Jason, for listening. For giving me a voice, even now, after all these years. Remember, the darkness does not define us, and there is always hope, even when it feels like there isn't. Though death might be calling to us, life is always a better option."

* * *

The moment the interview ended, Elena packed the mysterious box in her handbag, and left. Stunned, Jason sat in his chair, in the cold silence of his apartment, not moving. The

120

final words Anthony Bourdain had spoken rushed back at him. Bourdain's words echoed and rattled in his mind, not just as a conversation, but as a warning. Jason had opened a door to the other side, but he couldn't shake the feeling that something else was stepping through.

Lifting his finger he pressed STOP on the recording and saved the audio file. Then he stood; he needed to escape, to get out of his dark and airless apartment. He felt haunted, ashamed of the craving need for celebrity behind his questions about death. More than anything he needed to ease the pressure of shame and guilt building in his brain. There was only one person he could share this with.

His conscience racing, needing clarity, Jason snatched up his coat, then raced down the stairwell to catch up with Elena.

Stepping outside, Jason scanned the wind-blown street. It was four o'clock in the afternoon. He scratched the back of his neck, staring up and down the neighborhood, searching for Elena, only seeing a garbage truck pop out of an alleyway, the truck thundering past him in a roaring swish. Across the street he saw a stray dog sleeping alone on the shabby sidewalk. Nearby, a man with a long beard, a gray ponytail and a dented porkpie hat stood begging for coins in front of the blood bank.

Jason pursed his lips, ready to crumble. At the sharp click of heels at his back, he whirled to see Elena, rounding a downtown corner and heading south.

"Elena!" he yelled, and followed behind with his coattails flying.

Hearing Jason's voice, then watching him scampering up behind, Elena stopped. "You called, Jason?" she sighed.

Reaching her, caught his breath. He stood tall in respect, then lowered his head. Elena's eyes narrowed, seeming confused by this. "You wanted to say something?"

"Elena, yes," Jason fought for breath, his face flushed. *Where to start?* "Elena, I…I'm sorry. I want to apologize. I should have consulted you about the question I was planning to ask Tony. We…" He paused; *How to say this?* "We're a team, you and I. Without you, none of this is possible. And I wanted to confess — that is, to *share* — my gratitude. For all you've done. And…" he gulped, then said smiling coyly, "…to apologize for ever doubting you…doubting that you could do what you said you could."

Elena's accusing eyes stared him down. "What you mean to say, Jason, is that hearing the truth is not the same as seeing it."

Jason's smile wilted. "Yes," he said uncertainly, his pulse quickening.

They stood on the street, not speaking. In that moment, Jason saw the toll these interviews had taken on Elena. She looked like she'd aged a decade just in the past hour. Deep lines etched across her face; cracks and creases beginning to frame her sunken eyes; her long elegant neck now hunched forward. Jason was startled. The ache of wanting to understand what she was putting herself through filled him.

"Are you okay, Elena? You look like hell." He attempted to look sympathetic.

Elena bowed her head, the wide brim of her hat concealing her face.

"Channeling the dead isn't exactly a spa day, Jason. The dead take more than they give."

"Then why do you keep doing it?"

Elena looked up, eyebrows raised in astonishment. "Because someone has to. And because the voices of the unheard are worth the pain."

Instantly the color drained from Jason's face. For a moment he felt a tinge of panic. He reached out to put a comforting hand on Elena's arm, but she pushed it away. Staring in her eyes, Jason had never felt so dreadfully alone.

"You're opening doors, Jason," Elena said, a sad gleam in her eyes. "Make sure you're ready for what steps through. Some doors," she warned, and Jason felt a foreboding note of fear in her voice, "can't be closed once they're open. So beware. The dead don't rest. And neither will you."

CHAPTER EIGHT

Over the Edge, Into the Abyss

The abyss gazes back with hungry eyes.

Two days later, Jason woke gasping, his sheets tangled around his neck like iron chains, his stomach churning with a sickening twist of dread. Fingers clutching his pillow, wracked by agonizing gut pains, vomiting up bile and blood, he twisted and turned in bed, then stumbled into the bathroom, his heart hammering. Stripping off his sweaty pajamas he crawled into the shower, moaning and groaning until the pain slowly subsided.

What's going on? he wondered, squirming and shivering under the cold water. The pain continued assaulting him, sweat pouring out. It was as if his body knew what his mind refused to admit: today, he would be staring into the abyss, and the abyss would be staring back. His mind bombarded him with worries about today's podcast — what was sure to be the most challenging *Echoes* podcast thus far. He'd be speaking with

Sylvia Plath — a legendary poet and writer whose iconic book *The Bell Jar* had both inspired and haunted Jason. It was an opportunity Jason had longed for, hoping to understand how this writer had tried to heal her inner wounds using the power of words. Speaking with Plath was a moment he'd yearned for, ached for.

Yet he feared it with every fiber of his being.

Trying to suppress the fear did no good. The fear was embedded deep in Jason's core. It harkened back to his own suicidal thoughts, and the darkness and despair he had so long tried to conceal and escape. He had spent years burying the darker parts of himself — the nights when the weight of existence felt unbearable, the mornings when hope was a foreign concept. Sylvia Plath's words had always resonated too deeply, like an echo of his own pain. Today, he wasn't just speaking to her. He was speaking to the part of himself he feared the most. The part that lived in never-ending, hopeless despair.

Plath represented the ultimate manifestation of that despair, that last desperate dance with the darkness. Speaking with her would force him to face the part of himself that struggled with severe depression and rejection, that had been toying with the idea of giving up — on the podcast, on life, on himself. On everything.

Sylvia Plath. The name alone made Jason's stomach twist in knots of anxiety. Sure, he'd spoken with the troubled madman painter van Gogh, and the dangerously depressed Robin Williams — but there was something different about Plath. Maybe it was the fact that as an artist, she was unafraid to confront her own despair. Maybe it was that Plath's despair felt too familiar, too intimate, too close. He wasn't sure he could face her without facing the darker truth about himself — for this was the part of Jason that was only one short step away from stepping over the edge, into the abyss.

As the hour of the interview approached, Jason felt a hair-trigger of anxiety. He found himself unable to even crawl out of the shower, sitting with his back against the tile wall, knees up, curled into a ball of fear. For an hour he remained this way. A few times he found himself crying, struggling to hold onto control.

Finally stumbling back into bed, and pulling the covers over his head, Jason was plagued by dreams. In them, he stood before a closed door, its edges flickering like flame. On the other side, he knew that Sylvia Plath was waiting for him. "Come in," her mournful voice whispered, pulling him forward with a gravity he couldn't resist. He hesitated, placing his trembling hand on the knob, heart racing, a burning blur of pain in his chest. He desperately wanted to let go of the doorknob. But he couldn't. And so his clammy hand gripped it tight, and he waited. And waited. Waiting seemed part of the punishment.

* * *

Time for the interview arrived. The sun had long since dipped below the horizon, casting Jason's apartment into a murky gloom that mirrored the oppressive fog in his brain, the heaviness in his chest. A single lamp on his desk flickered weakly, illuminating the stack of research books beside it — Sylvia Plath's *The Bell Jar*, *Ariel*, and collections of her letters and poems.

Opening his laptop, Jason sucked in a deep breath, put a rise into his shoulders. He motioned for Elena to take a seat as he concentrated on looking confident. Elena settled into the chair opposite him, placing the carved wooden box between them, her eyes closed in concentration as she prepared to channel Sylvia Plath.

Jason's fingers hovered over the RECORD button, trembling. He forced himself to breathe, reminding himself that this was just another interview. Just another podcast. But deep down, he knew it wasn't. This was a conversation with a voice from the void, with a soul who had walked too closely with despair, who had stepped over the edge and fallen.

The air in the room grew dense, thick, suffocating, pressing down on Jason like an invisible weight. Shadows lengthened unnaturally, the desk light flashing bright then flickering as if something unseen was siphoning its strength. Jason watched as Elena's features softened, her expression melting into one of profound melancholy that Jason instantly recognized from photographs of Plath, her eyes darkening into pools of sadness. When Elena's lips parted and she finally spoke, the voice was gentle yet laced with sorrow, a sound that sent chills racing up Jason's spine and made the hairs on the back of his neck stand on end.

"Hello, Jason," Sylvia said, her voice barely more than a breath.

Jason swallowed hard, his throat tight. His head throbbed. He reached out to press STOP on the recording button, then composed himself, and leaned closer to the microphone.

"Hello, Sylvia," he managed, his voice faltering. "It's an honor to speak with you. Your work…your writing…it's meant so much to so many, including me." He closed his eyes tight, shading them from the glowing laptop screen.

"Thank you," Sylvia Plath replied, the sadness in her voice palpable. "I'm glad my words have found a place in the hearts of others, even though they were born from such heartache, such pain."

Jason nodded, his chest constricting. Opening his eyes, he breathed deeply to calm himself. "Your writing... it's so raw, so painfully, brutally honest. It feels like you were pouring your very soul onto the page. Was it like that for you?"

"Yes," Sylvia's voice was soft but unwavering. "Writing was my only way to make sense of the chaos within. It was a lifeline. But it was also a curse. The more I wrote, the deeper I delved into my own darkness, my self-damnation, and the harder it became to find my way back to the light...

"Words were my sanctuary, Jason, my refuge from the storm raging inside. But they were also my tormentors, dragging me into the darkest depths of myself, exposing wounds I didn't know how to heal.'"

Jason nodded, feeling the conversation going into forbidden territory — so profoundly off-limits that it frightened him. "Your work often explores the struggle with identity, particularly the tension between societal expectations and personal self-discovery. Did you feel like these external pressures were a barrier to finding your true self?"

A sigh escaped Elena's lips, Sylvia's voice filled with a weariness that seemed to echo through the room. "Absolutely. My book *The Bell Jar* was my attempt to capture that struggle — the suffocating pressure to conform, to be the perfect woman, the perfect wife, the perfect mother — while every minute of the day feeling chained in Hell and wanting only one thing: to die. The world pressured me to be perfect, Jason. But perfection is a lie — a cage they build around you until you forget how to breathe. I wasn't a woman to anyone. I was a reflection of what everybody in my life wanted to see. Inside, I was grappling with who I really was, separate from those expectations. It felt like I was trapped beneath a bell jar, gasping for the air of freedom, suffocating in a world that refused to see me as I truly was…

"*The Bell Jar* wasn't just my shriek of depression. It was the silence that surrounded it — the suffocating weight of being unseen, unheard, even as I screamed through every line I wrote. Every word I unleashed was a plea, a prayer for resurrection. I wanted to rise, Jason, like Lady Lazarus. But resurrection comes with its own weight — the memory of the grave never leaves you."

Listening to her, Jason felt an unsettling clarity. He had spent so much of his life chasing approval, contorting himself into shapes he thought others wanted. Hearing Sylvia's words was like gazing into a mirror, showing him the cracks he had tried so hard to hide and ignore. "The bell jar... it's such a powerful metaphor. It represents not just the suffocation of your identity, but also the suffocating nature of mental illness. How did you see the relationship between these two?"

Sylvia's voice grew distant, as if she were peering into the depths of her own mind. "The bell jar was my depression. It trapped me, isolated me, made the world feel distant and unreachable. I wanted to escape it, but the more I struggled, the tighter it seemed to close around me. It was a prison of my own mind, a barrier that kept me from living, from breathing freely."

Jason's heart ached with the depth of her despair. "And the stigma...the way society viewed mental illness at the time — how did that affect you?"

"It was an additional weight," Sylvia replied, her voice tinged with bitterness. "People didn't understand, and that lack of understanding only deepened the isolation. The stigma made it harder to seek help, harder to even admit that I needed it. I felt like a failure, not just as a woman, or a writer, but as a person, because I couldn't live up to what was expected of me."

Jason could feel the intensity of her words, the raw honesty that had made Plath's work resonate so deeply with readers. It made it hard not to weep in his own agony, replaying morbid thoughts that never seemed to go away. "In your poetry, especially in pieces like *Lady Lazarus* and *Ariel*, you explored the concept of death and rebirth. How did those themes reflect your personal journey?"

"Death and rebirth were intertwined in my mind," Sylvia answered, her voice growing softer, reflective. "I saw death as a release, a way to escape the confines of my identity, of the expectations that strangled me. But there was also a part of me that yearned for rebirth, for transformation. In *Lady Lazarus*, I wrote about the idea of rising again, of coming back stronger, even after being destroyed. It was both a literal and metaphorical struggle — the desire to break free, to be reborn, yet knowing that the cycle would continue, that the darkness would return."

Jason nodded slowly, absorbing her words. "It's as if the act of creation, of writing, was a way for you to confront mortality, to engage with it directly."

"Yes," Sylvia said, her voice filled with a quiet resolve. "Writing was my way of facing my fears, of giving form to the chaos within. In poems like *Daddy* and *Edge*, I confronted death, not as an abstract concept, but as something real, tangible, something that had a presence in my life. It was my way of making sense of it, of trying to find some kind of peace, even if that peace was fleeting."

"Did you ever find any relief in writing? Any sense of peace?"

"There were moments," Sylvia replied, as if the words resisted coming, and squirmed out of her heart. "Moments when the act of creation gave me a sense of purpose, a sense of control. But they were always short-lived. The darkness never stayed away for long. It was like I was always on the edge, teetering between life and death, between hope and despair…

"'Despair is a quiet thing. It doesn't shout. It whispers, creeping in when you're most vulnerable, convincing you it's the only truth. But it's a liar."

The words sliced through Jason's mind. Suddenly he felt woozy with fear, the pain in his stomach returning. He stared at his watch, praying it was time to stop. Then he focused his eyes on the ceiling, while his heart fluttered. "Did you ever feel like there was no escape, like you were trapped by the roles society imposed on you?"

"Yes, Jason," Sylvia answered. "I was expected to be everything to everyone, including my readers and my publishers, to other writers and other poets — and yet I felt like I was failing at all of it. I couldn't see a way out."

Jason closed his eyes, trying to imagine the crushing sense of hopelessness she must have felt. "And that's when you decided…" he paused, anxious, holding back tears…*God, please help me!* "…that it was time to end your life?"

"Yes," Sylvia replied. "I felt like I had no choice. The darkness had engulfed me, swallowed me whole, and I couldn't see any other way to escape it. I felt I was dragging everybody else down with me. I thought…I thought it would be better for everyone if I were gone. That I was a burden, that the world would be better off without me. The only way out of the darkness is through it. And no one makes it through alone."

Jason's throat tightened, the tears he had been holding back finally spilling over. "Sylvia…I'm so sorry. I'm sorry that you felt that way, that you felt so alone."

"Thank you, Jason," Sylvia said, her voice trembling with emotion. "But it's too late for me. My story is over. What matters now is what others like you take from it. I hope…I hope they can see that they are not alone, that there is always another way, even when it feels like there isn't."

Jason nodded, wiping at his eyes. "Your words have saved so many people, Sylvia. They've given hope to those who are struggling, those who feel like they can't go on. Your legacy is one of strength, of resilience, of..." Suddenly he couldn't go on, fighting back emotions, tortured by years of self-punishment, praying for help. *When does it end, God? When does it end?*

There was a pause, and when Sylvia spoke again, her voice was now a murmur, a wail. "I wish I could have seen that in life. But I'm glad…I'm glad that my words have found a home in the hearts of others, that they have given others the strength that I couldn't find in myself."

Jason felt his heart break for her, for the life that had been lost too soon. "If you could go back, if you could change anything, what would you do differently?"

Sylvia's voice grew soft, wistful. "I would have tried to reach out, to let others in, to let them see the pain I was in. But I was so afraid of being seen as weak, fragile, a disappointment, a failure. I kept everything inside, and it became a blazing fire that consumed me. If I could go back, I would have allowed myself to be vulnerable, to ask for help."

Jason nodded, his heart heavy. "Thank you, Sylvia. Thank you for sharing your story, for being so open, so honest."

"Thank you, Jason," Sylvia replied, her voice filled with a deep sense of gratitude. "For listening, for giving me a voice. I hope...I hope my words can continue to help others, even now."

Jason took a deep breath, the enormity of the conversation they had just had squeezing him. He felt torn; he knew this was the moment to ask the question that had been weighing on him throughout the interview, the same question he'd asked Anthony Bourdain — the question that had turned Tony's anger back outward at him.

"Sylvia," he began, his heart trembling, "can we talk more about your death? Your suicide?" As soon as Jason asked the question, he felt uncomfortable, his mind swirling with worry.

"What would you like to know?" Sylvia's voice was soft, musical, even while discussing how she succumbed to her inner demons.

Jason paused, cleared his throat. "Why did you choose death?"

"I knew death too well. The darkness...it never left me." Sylvia's voice murmured through Elena's lips. "It stayed with me, no matter how hard I tried to fight it. My writing...it was just a way to make sense of the chaos. It was only ever a way to slow the darkness. Words never really healed the pain. In the end, writing wasn't enough. Nothing was. I was already too far gone…

"Suicide wasn't a decision, Jason. It was a surrender. The darkness had been my companion for so long, promising that the pain would end if I let it. And in that moment, I believed it. But I didn't think about the echoes I would leave behind — the children, the friends, the readers who would carry my absence like a stone in their hearts. If I could go back, I would have screamed for help, shattered the silence that kept me bound. But fear is a powerful thing, Jason. It makes you believe the lie that you're alone.'"

Jason's chest tightened, the air in the room too thin. He wasn't just hearing Sylvia's story — he was living it, every word peeling back the layers of his own despair. He had thought the podcast would save him, but now he wondered if it was only leading him closer to the edge "Is that what it feels like?" he asked. "That lack of hope? That nothing can ever be enough?"

"You know it is, Jason," Sylvia replied. "You've felt it, too."

Suddenly across the table Elena jerked back, rising in her chair, as if coming awake. Her eyelids fluttered, her hands reached out blindly for the carved box. Seeing this, Jason willed his mind to hurry. To let Sylvia Plath pass back into her dreamless sleep.

"Sylvia," Jason began softly, "what message would you give to young listeners who might be going through a rough patch in their lives? What would you say to them?"

"Life can be unbearable," Sylvia said, her voice filled with a gentle yet urgent compassion. "The pressures of the world, of expectations, of fear and loneliness, can feel like it's too much to carry. But stepping into the abyss, embracing the siren song of death and extinguishing your life, doesn't solve anything. Yes, life is cruel. Life will break your heart. But life is also full of bright hope and good will. I once wrote a love song to life. It went: *'I shut my eyes and all the world drops dead; I lift my lids and all is born again...'*

"The darkness doesn't offer us peace, Jason. It offers us lies, tells us that we're alone, that the pain will never end. But even in the abyss, plunged into absolute darkness, there is light. You just have to hold on long enough to see it. My words were my way of fighting the darkness. They didn't save me, but maybe they can save someone else. And that, Jason, is enough."

Jason felt a deep connection to Sylvia in that moment, a shared understanding of the struggles they both faced. "Thank you, Sylvia. I will make sure your message reaches them."

Pressing STOP on the recording, Jason sat perched on the edge of his chair. Elena's eyes were open, no longer channeling. She let out a breath slowly. *God, she looks drained!* Jason realized in horror. *Even more exhausted than before!* The creases and cracks around Elena's eyes had deepened, locks of hair Jason hadn't noticed before turning gray, some white.

Sylvia Plath's words hung in the air, a testament to the pain she had carried and the strength she had found in sharing it. Jason had expected to hear about her struggles, her pain, her anguish, but what he hadn't anticipated was the profound sense of compassion and connection he now felt — to Sylvia Plath, to his own work, and to the countless others who had ever felt lost in the dark.

The conversation had touched him in ways he hadn't expected, leaving him with a deeper understanding of the fragility of the human soul and the resilience that lies within it. As he typed out a title for the audio file, and shut down his laptop, Jason knew that this was a story that needed to be told — a story that could save others, hoping it could also save him.

Ushering Elena silently from the apartment, Jason was surprised to see it was the dead of night. He locked and bolted the door, letting a wave of nausea pass. He felt lightheaded. *You need to eat something,* he decided, his guts lurching, tied in knots. He headed to the kitchen, searched the humming refrigerator for a frozen TV dinner, then turned on the oven, all the while staring across the room at the recording device. Sylvia's words still echoed in his mind. He had always thought of himself as the interviewer, the one seeking answers. But now he realized he was the subject, and the question he was asking was whether he had the strength to keep going. *Do I?* he wondered. He had faced his fears and spoken with Sylvia Plath, but it felt like he had spoken with himself — the part of him he had been running from. And for the first time, he wasn't sure if he could outrun it.

As the oven warmed, Jason went to the window and stared out into the chill darkness. *This is a turning point,* he realized. This time, death had touched him. He'd been walking a blurry line between despair and hope, between the abyss and survival. Going forward, that line would sharpen, and Jason would need to pick a side. *Death? Life?* In speaking with the dead, he would be walking the dangerous edge of madness — just like Sylvia Plath had.

And she hadn't made it back, Jason reminded himself. *What if I can't either?*

CHAPTER NINE

The Dark Star, Flaming Bright

Dark stars burn brightest before they fall.□

Adrenaline coursing through his veins, Jason stayed holed up in his apartment for two days, deliriously preparing notes for his podcast. Selecting the next interview with the dead would be a crucial turning point, if *Echoes* was to go viral. He'd already decided to speak with a musician. To boost his podcast, however, he needed one whose death was shrouded with controversy. One whose life was a march through Hell marked by pain, anguish, heartache, maybe even addictions. A star whose fire had flamed out; the music world's darkest falling star.

The trouble was, there were many — tragic figures like Elvis and Janis and Jimi, John Lennon and Jim Morrison and Freddie Mercury, Michael Jackson and Prince, Tupac and Whitney Houston.

A frown creased Jason's face. Trying to decide depressed his spirits. Suddenly he sat back in shock, his mind reeling, as a name raced to his feverish brain.

Kurt. Kurt Cobain. Of course!

Startled by this brainstorm, Jason fumbled to find his journal to scribble down some notes. Yet even as he jotted a list of questions, his heart burning with love for Cobain's music, the idea suddenly sent a shock of intense dread. Even flipping through his stack of Nirvana CDs and record albums, and pulling out *Bleach* and *In Utero* and *Nevermind*, gave Jason no relief.

Kurt Cobain. The name chilled him. It evoked a legacy of anguish, rebellion, and a violent tragic end. Kurt had been the voice of a generation, a living symbol of disillusionment and frustration that many felt but could never quite articulate. His tortured songs, with their raw energy and sarcastic, biting lyrics, had captured the hearts of millions of disaffected listeners. Yet behind the fame and adoration was a man who had struggled with his own demons, who'd suffered a childhood of rejection and abandonment, a decade of teenage depression and drug addictions. A young man who had ultimately chosen to silence his remarkable voice forever in one blast of a shotgun.

*　*　*

Fame devours its children in precise increments, bite by measured bite. Jason understood this now, watching Elena channel the voice of Kurt Cobain, in the hollow hours before dawn, when the world felt thin enough for truth to slip through its cracks. His apartment had become a confessional booth, the soft red glow of Jason's recording equipment painting everything in the pulsing colors of bruised lesions, old wounds, old scars.

The wooden box between Jason and Elena pulsed with its own inner light, like a heart beating beneath ancient wood. Each throb and thrum drew more substance from Elena, her black-cloaked figure already beginning to blur at the edges like a photograph left too long in the blistering sunlight. Her transformation had begun the moment she closed her eyes — not the theatrical possession he'd half-expected, but something more subtle and terrifying. It was as if she were being slowly erased, becoming transparent enough for someone else's soul to shine through.

The pre-dawn air hung heavy with invisible rain, carrying the misty ghost of Seattle's perpetual drizzle, though they were thousands of miles from the city where Kurt had last drawn breath. Through the windows, streetlights flickered like dying

144

stars, their glow catching the empty liquor bottles that lined Jason's walls — sentinels marking nights spent trying to drown out the voices of both living and dead.

Jason creaked back and forth uneasily in his chair. His hands trembling, he adjusted the microphone, then clicked the RECORD button. No amount of preparation could ease the knot of anxiety tightening in his gut. This wasn't just another episode of *Echoes*; this was a journey into the mind and heart of a young man who had lived on the razor's edge, beloved by millions, driven by powerful self-hatred, who had crawled through every inch of Purgatory in an effort to extinguish himself.

Nervously Jason peered across the kitchen table. Watching Elena's features morph into a look of deep sadness made his heart ache. When she spoke, the voice that emerged from Elena's lips was not hers, but Kurt's — soft, weary, and tinged with bitterness. A voice that carried all the weight of heroin dreams and guitar feedback.

"Hey, man," Kurt slurred, his speech raw and raspy, as if he had been screaming for hours.

Jason felt a lump form in his throat, his hands shaking as he gripped the edge of the desk. "Kurt…hello. It's an honor. Thank you so much for being here."

Kurt let out a bitter laugh. Jason hesitated, unsure how to respond. He had always been a fan of Cobain and Nirvana, drawn to Kurt's identity as a misfit, and the scalding emotion in their songs. But now, faced with the man himself, he felt unprepared for the depth of the pain that lay thumping like a drum beat beneath the surface.

"Kurt," Jason began again carefully, "your songs…Nirvana's music…it spoke to so many people. It gave voice to a generation that felt lost, angry, and misunderstood. Songs like 'Come As You Are,' 'Lithium,' 'Smells Like Teen Spirit,' and 'Heart-Shaped Box.' But I know every word came from a place of intense pain. Physical pain. Emotional pain. Can you tell me what it was like, living with that pain?"

A long pause followed, the silence in the room suffocating. "Pain…yeah, dude, that pretty much sums it up," Kurt answered. "It was like this constant weight on my chest, that 'voice of a generation' bullshit, this feeling that no matter what I did, the pressure and the pain would never go away. Music…that was my only way of coping, my way of screaming into the void. But the void doesn't scream back, Jason. It just swallows you whole."

Jason's heart clenched at the words, the despair in Kurt's voice almost too much to bear. "Did the music help at all? Did it give you any relief?"

Kurt let out another bitter laugh. "Relief? Not really. The drugs did. Heroin did. But even drugs became more like a distraction, something to keep me from thinking about how fucked up everything was. But the thing is, when the music stops, the negative thoughts come roaring back. And they're louder than ever."

Kurt's voice grew more somber, pressing down on him. "There were times when it felt like I was trapped, like there was no way to escape the pain. Sometimes solutions get all twisted up in the confusion of doing what's right, when everything inside you says to do what's wrong. Sometimes goodbye's the only way. It's a painful realization — but, man, it's the truth. 'When life leaves us blind, love keeps us kind,' my wife Courtney always said. But even love can't always save you from yourself."

Jason nodded, understanding. "You once wrote, in the song 'Lithium,' '*I'm so happy because today I found my friends — they're in my head.*' Did you feel like you were alone, even when you were surrounded by thousands of people who loved you?"

A note of sadness crept into Kurt's voice. "Hell yeah, man, I did. I always felt like there was this distance between me and everyone else, like I was living in a different reality. People would try to reach out, try to help, but it was like the real Kurt was invisible, and all they saw was the guy screaming on a stage, the big, rich rock n' roll star. They couldn't see the real me, the part of me that was falling apart. I felt like I was screaming for help, but no one could hear me."

Jason felt tears prick at the corners of his eyes. "Did you ever feel like you could open up, like you could let people in?"

Kurt sighed, the sound filled with regret. "I wanted to, Jason. I really did. But it's hard, you know? When you're the one who's supposed to be the strong one, the leader, the one who's supposed to have all the answers. You start to think that maybe you don't deserve the help, that you're supposed to be strong enough to handle it on your own. And when you can't…trust me, it just makes the pain worse…

"You know that Neil Young line I scribbled in my suicide note? *'It's better to burn out than to fade away'*? That haunts me now. It haunts the living shit out of me — almost as much as leaving my little girl Frances behind. And I know it's haunted and fucked with Neil Young his entire life…

"You want to know about death?" Kurt asked. The words almost sprang at Jason, snarling. "Or do you want to know about fame? Because they're the same thing, really. Both ways of disappearing while everyone watches. Both ways of dying in public, piece by piece, until there's nothing left but other people's ideas of who you were supposed to be."

Jason leaned forward, fingers tightening on his microphone. This wasn't the angry punk rocker he'd expected. This was something else — something that cut closer to the bone. The voice carried echoes of late-night conversations and bitter truths, the kind of honesty that only comes when fame's spotlight has burned away all pretense.

"Tell me what you mean," Jason managed, trying to keep his voice steady. He could hear his heart pounding an ocean in his ears, as across the table Elena's skin took on the alabaster translucence of funeral parlor makeup.

Again Kurt's bitter laugh echoed through the room. It was the same laugh that had punctuated interviews with journalists when questions got too close to truth. "Fame is like a spotlight that casts the darkest shadows. The brighter it gets, the deeper the darkness grows behind you. Eventually, you start to think maybe the darkness is all there is — that maybe it's all there ever was. And the worst part? The darkness starts feeling like home. Like the only real thing left in a world of sold-out arenas and camera flashes and screaming faces that want pieces of you until there's nothing left to take."

Jason nodded, then his gaze drifted back to Elena. Elena's hands trembled on the wooden conduit box, her veins visible through skin that had become like tissue paper. For a moment Jason thought of turning off the recorder. But Kurt's voice continued, gaining strength with each word, as if finally finding the language for truths he'd never managed to express in life.

"You know what's funny?" The voice became more intimate, like the secret confessions between songs at *MTV Unplugged* sessions. "Everyone thinks 'Smells Like Teen Spirit' was about rebellion. But it wasn't. It was about fear. Fear of being seen. Fear of not being seen. Fear that maybe you're not really there at all — that maybe you're just a collection of other people's expectations wearing your face."

Jason felt something shift in the air — not a temperature drop, but a squeezing, a pressing in, as if the darkness itself were leaning closer to listen. The walls of his apartment seemed to distort, and the ceiling to breathe, expanding and contracting with each word, like a lung taking in poison and exhaling truth.

"Is that why you..." Jason started to ask, but Kurt cut him off with a sharpness that felt like guitar strings snapping.

"Why I ate a shotgun? Put the period at the end of my own sentence?" There was no anger in the voice now, only a terrible clarity. "Everyone thinks they know why. They blame the drugs, the fame, the pressure. But here's the truth — man, I died long before I pulled that trigger. Fame just preserved the corpse for a while, kept it dancing for the cameras until even the strings holding me up started to rot."

Feeling an icy chill in the room, Jason wrapped his arms around himself. Elena made a small sound, something between a gasp and a whimper. Blood-red tears traced down her cheeks, but the voice that emerged from her throat was still Kurt's, carrying all the gloomy melancholy of Seattle rain and broken promises.

"You know what your problem is, Jason?" Kurt abruptly said. The question paralyzed Jason in his chair. "You're chasing ghosts. Like I did. Like we all do. But you want to know the real tragedy? The ghosts are chasing you, too. And they're hungry. So fucking hungry."

The words hung in the air like smoke from a last cigarette. Jason felt them settle into his bones, carrying the burden of truth he'd been trying to outrun since Judith's death.

"I don't understand," he mumbled, but even as the words left his mouth, he knew they were a lie. The kind of lie fame tells itself in mirror-bright dressing rooms. The kind of lie grief promises in the dark.

"Yeah, you do," Kurt said. "You're not really talking to me. You're not talking to any of us. You're talking to *her*. To Judith. Using our voices to drown out the one voice you can't bear to hear — your own."

The name hit Jason like feedback through blown speakers. *How does he know about Judith?* The thought disturbed him. He suddenly noticed his teeth were clenched tight. Meanwhile he watched Elena's face contort in pain, as if the truth were something sharp working its way through her increasingly transparent flesh.

"The dead know things," Kurt continued. "We see the remorse that's gnawing at you, the guilt that's eating you alive. You think these interviews with the dead are about giving voice to the voiceless? Bullshit. They're about asking yourself why *you* survived when she didn't."

Elena's hand shot out suddenly, grabbing Jason's wrist. Jason flinched. *What's happening?!* Her skin felt like Seattle winter, but her grip crunched down like the steel jaws of a bear trap. When she opened her eyes, they were still sea-green, but ancient with borrowed pain.

"He's right," Elena whispered, her voice her own again but somehow different—hollowed out like an empty stage after the last encore. "I should know, Jason. I lost someone too. That's why I started this. Why I learned to open the door between worlds. But the dead..." She drew a shuddering breath that seemed to rattle through her increasingly visible bones. "I warned you before, Jason. The dead take more than they give. Each time we open that door, they take another piece of us with them when that door closes."

Jason stared at her hand on his wrist, really seeing for the first time how thin her skin had become, how the blue veins mapped a geography of loss beneath the surface. Like track marks on the arm of someone who'd learned to mainline grief.

"Elena, I —"

"Don't apologize." She cut him off with the finality of a power chord. "Just listen. Kurt's trying to tell you something important. Something I learned too late."

Bewildered, Jason raised his eyebrows, then snatched his hand away from her. The voice that came next was Kurt's again, but layered with Elena's exhaustion. "The dead don't need a voice. They need peace," Kurt said. "Just like you do."

Jason listened, in shock. Tears welled in his eyes. Elena slumped back in her chair, her body drained, her eyes closed. For a heartbeat Jason studied her. In the gray light of approaching dawn, he could see new streaks of white in her hair, as if the conversation had aged her years in minutes. As if fame and death were finally finishing what they'd started.

"We have to stop," Jason said urgently, the words surprising him even as they left his mouth.

Elena's eyes snapped open. She searched Jason's face, then shook her head, gathering up the wooden box with trembling hands. "It's too late for that. The door's already open. And the dead..." She looked at him with eyes that had seen too much. "They're hungry for more than just stories now."

She stood unsteadily, like a rock star after too many encores. Jason reached out for her, but she pushed past. At the door, she paused, looking back at him with an expression that mixed pity and understanding.

"Fame and death, Jason. Kurt was right; they're the same thing. Both ways of disappearing while everyone watches. Remember that before you upload this interview."

She gave Jason a long chilling look. Then the door closed behind her with a click that somehow sounded final as a gunshot. Jason sat alone in the growing dawn, the recorder still running. He reached to turn it off, but stopped when he heard something — a hush beneath the room tone, almost too quiet to hear.

Squinting his eyes, Jason listened. It was Kurt's voice, or maybe Elena's, or maybe his own: "The ghosts are always listening. And they remember everything we're trying to forget."

Jason nearly leaped out of his chair. He hit the STOP button, hands shaking. On his laptop screen, the sound waves from the interview pulsed and throbbed like a heartbeat. Or like something taking its last breath.

Outside his window, the city was waking, the day becoming sunny and hot. But in his apartment, the gloom seemed deeper than before. And somewhere in there, he could have sworn he heard someone humming the opening notes to "Come As You Are" — that song about fate, and memory, and the impossibility of escape.

The same song that had been playing on the radio the morning Judith died.

Pressing SAVE on the recording, Jason let out a long sigh. The universe, it seemed, had a cruel sense of irony. Or maybe it was just Kurt's ghost, teaching him one final lesson about the price of turning pain into art, and art into echoes that would outlive them all.

Fame devours its children.

But grief? Jason thought to himself.

Grief makes them immortal.

CHAPTER TEN

The Voice of the Broken

Light bleeds through the cracks we cannot mend.

The street was eerily dark as Elena climbed the stairs and entered Jason's apartment. She sat in the dimly-lit kitchen, while Jason paced the moonshadowed floor. Silhouettes danced restlessly on the walls. His mind still buzzed with the echoes of past conversations, where he had delved into the souls of history's most influential figures. Each encounter had left a mark on him, expanding his understanding of the human condition in ways he never thought possible. The last two — Sylvia Plath and Kurt Cobain — had scarred him. Tonight, however, he was about to converse with an absolute superstar, a woman whose life had been an enigma, a symbol of both dazzling sexual beauty and deep vulnerability — Marilyn Monroe.

Monroe wasn't just a Hollywood star; she was an icon, a paradox wrapped in the trappings of fame and fragility. Over the past days, Jason had submerged himself in her films, devoured her biographies, and contemplated the countless images of this blonde bombshell that had seared themselves into the collective memory. He knew this conversation would be unlike any other — more intimate, more revealing.

Now it was midnight. Jason took his seat at the kitchen table, pursed his lips thoughtfully, then pressed the RECORD button. As Elena began to channel Marilyn Monroe, the room became icy, her breathing deliberate, her eyes fluttering closed as the apartment became charged with electricity. Jason watched as Elena's features softened, transforming into an almost ethereal reflection of the woman they were about to speak with. When she spoke, the voice that emerged was unmistakably Marilyn's — soft, breathy, laced with a sadness that felt almost tangible.

"Hello, Jason," Marilyn's voice greeted him. "It's nice to be here."

Jason offered a small, sad smile, feeling an ache deep in his chest. "Marilyn, hello. You've touched so many lives, including mine. But I know your life wasn't always as glamorous as it appeared. Can you share what it was like to live under the world's gaze, with the image the world had of you?"

The silence that followed was heavy, filled with unspoken sorrow. "It was...lonely," Marilyn answered. "People saw me as this beautiful, glamorous movie star, but they didn't see the real me. Beneath the makeup, behind the smile, I was just a girl who wanted the world. I felt like I was always playing a role, always trying to be what people wanted me to be. But inside, I was struggling...struggling to find myself."

Jason felt a pang of empathy, his heart breaking for the woman adored by millions yet so isolated in her own skin. "You once said, 'I'm trying to find myself. Sometimes that's not easy.' Did you feel that people never really understood you?"

Marilyn's voice softened, tinged with a quiet resignation. "Yes, I think that's true. I was always trying to be perfect, to live up to the expectations everyone had of me. But I wasn't perfect, Jason. I was flawed, just like everyone else. Sometimes, I felt like my whole life was one big rejection...like no matter what I did, I could never be good enough. It was hard...really hard."

Jason nodded, feeling the depth of her struggle. "You've also said, 'Sometimes I feel my whole life has been one big rejection.' Did you ever find solace in solitude, in being alone with your thoughts?"

A sigh escaped Marilyn. "I tried to, Jason. I really did. But being alone...it was hard for me. I craved love, attention, validation...but at the same time, I was terrified of letting people get too close. I didn't want them to see the real me, the girl who was insecure, who didn't always have it together. So I pushed people away, even when I didn't want to. It was a constant struggle…wanting to be loved but being afraid of what that love might reveal."

Jason's voice softened, sensing the truth of her words. "You once said, 'I believe that everything happens for a reason. People change so that you can learn to let go, things go wrong so that you appreciate them when they're right, you believe lies so you eventually learn to trust no one but yourself.' Did you find any comfort in this belief, in the idea that your experiences, as painful as they were, had a purpose?"

Marilyn's voice grew more contemplative, as if reflecting on a life filled with lessons. "I wanted to believe that, Jason. I really did. Life was full of ups and downs, and I tried to learn from each one, to grow stronger. But it was hard, and sometimes it was really hard to see the reason behind the pain. I craved love, but I also feared it. I was always learning, always growing, but I never felt like I truly found myself."

Jason felt the tension in the air, the rawness of the conversation touching his own vulnerabilities. "You also said, 'Fame doesn't fulfill you. It warms you a bit, but that warmth is temporary.' Did you ever feel like fame stole something from you, something you could never get back?"

Marilyn's voice was edged with bitterness. "It did. Fame…fame is a machine, Jason. It chews you up and spits you out, and it doesn't care who you are or what you're going through. It just wants more — more sex, more beauty, more glamour, more of whatever it can use to make money. I felt like I was always giving, always trying to be what they wanted, but it was never enough. And in the end…I lost a part of myself in the process."

Jason's thoughts turned to her words about ambition and success. "You also said, 'I don't want to make money. I just want to be wonderful.' What did being 'wonderful' mean to you?"

Marilyn's voice filled with a quiet longing. "Being wonderful… it meant being loved, being appreciated for who I was, not just for how I looked or what I could do for others. I wanted to be seen, truly seen, and valued for more than just my beauty. But I don't think I ever really found that…not in the way I wanted."

Jason felt his heart shatter for the woman who had given so much to the world, only to feel so unfulfilled in return.

"Marilyn, did fame ever bring you happiness, even for a moment?"

A soft, rueful laugh escaped Marilyn. "It's funny, isn't it? Fame warms you a bit, but that warmth is temporary. It doesn't fulfill you, not in the way people think it will. I thought that if I became famous, if people loved me, it would fill the emptiness inside. But it didn't. It just made me feel more isolated, more alone. Fame doesn't bring happiness, Jason. It just magnifies whatever you're already feeling… good or bad…

"When you're famous," she continued, "you run into human nature in a raw kind of way. It stirs up envy, and hatred. People you run into feel that, *Well, who is she, who does she think she is, Marilyn Monroe?* They think fame gives them some kind of privilege to walk up to you and say anything, and it won't hurt your feelings."

Hearing this, and thinking of his own dreams of fame, Jason's stomach went cold. Marilyn continued. "Fame has a special burden, which I might as well state here and now. I didn't mind being burdened with being glamorous and sexual. But what goes with it can be a burden. I feel that beauty and femininity are ageless and can't be contrived, and glamour can't be manufactured. Not real glamour, anyway; it's based on femininity. I think that sexuality is only attractive when it's

162

natural and spontaneous. This is where a lot of people miss the boat. We are all born sexual creatures, thank God, but it's a pity so many people despise and crush this natural gift. Art, real art, comes from it. Everything does.

"I never quite understood it, this sex symbol stuff. I always thought symbols were those things you clash together! That's the trouble: a sex symbol becomes a *thing*. I just hated to be a thing. But you asked about happiness...I was never used to being happy, so that wasn't something I ever took for granted. You see, I was brought up differently from the average child because the average child is brought up expecting to be happy. So happiness? I guess I never expected that. Maybe that's why it eluded me. Happiness scared me. Frankly, I'm grateful not to have to think about it anymore."

Jason could sense the depth of her pain and struggle. "You once said, 'Imperfection is beauty, madness is genius and it's better to be absolutely ridiculous than absolutely boring.' Did you ever feel like people truly understood what you meant by that?"

Marilyn's voice grew a touch brighter, as if remembering a belief that had carried her through difficult times. "I always felt like I was living in a world that tried to make everyone the same, Jason. But I knew that wasn't right. There's beauty in imperfection, in the little quirks that make us who we are. Madness, too — sometimes it's the only thing that makes sense in a world that often doesn't. I wanted people to see that it's okay to be different, to embrace who you are, even if it seems ridiculous to others."

Jason felt a lump form in his throat. "Marilyn…what advice would you give to someone who is struggling, who feels lost in the darkness? How did you keep going, even when it felt like the world was against you?"

Marilyn's voice grew softer, filled with quiet wisdom. "I'd tell them that it's okay to feel lost sometimes, that it's part of the journey. Life isn't always going to be easy, and there will be moments when you doubt yourself, when you feel like giving up. But it's important to hold on to the belief that everything happens for a reason, even if you can't see it at the time. And remember: it's okay to be vulnerable, to let people in, even when it's scary. That's where real strength comes from — not from pretending to be perfect, but from being honest about who you are and what you're going through."

CHAPTER ELEVEN

When the Dead Speak Louder Than the Living

Success tastes like ashes in a dead man's mouth.

Jason sat in the pre-dawn gloom of his apartment, the blue light of his laptop screen casting a corpse-glow across his face as the numbers for *Echoes* climbed relentlessly into the millions. Waiting all night to see the new listener numbers had set his teeth on edge. The Kurt Cobain podcast had done more than go viral — it had become viral in the way that plagues are viral. Spreading. Consuming. Transforming everything it touched into something darker, hungrier. His interview with Marilyn Monroe had gone beyond, doubling the number of *Echoes* listeners. The impact of this podcast stunned Jason, as he watched the number of downloads skyrocketing overnight. Ten million. Then fifteen million. The manner in which *Echoes* had taken the podcast world by storm was unprecedented, unparalleled; the reviews on CNN and Fox News were glowing with praise.

Even more passionate and glowing were the comments posted by *Echoes* listeners. Comments scrolled past Jason's eyes like digital confetti: "Groundbreaking journalism"..."Revolutionary storytelling"..."A voice for the voiceless." In addition to praise they posted messages of compassion and hope to each other. None of them understood what they were really praising — Jason's ability to mine graves for content, to transform private pain and anguish and tragedy into public entertainment. None of them saw the true cost of each downloaded shriek of anguish, each hushed prayer for peace from beyond.

For an hour, Jason sat at his laptop, reading and re-reading the reactions. Suddenly his phone vibrated against the desk — another media request, another chance to explain his "innovative approach to grief journalism." He ignored it, focusing instead on the message that had arrived precisely at 3:33 A.M., its timestamp a mockery of holy numbers:

St. Agnes. Come alone. The dead are hungry. - E

St. Agnes. Jason nodded, gulping air; he knew it well. The name itself was a ghost story waiting to be told. Everyone in the city knew its skeleton — the abandoned and crumbling Gothic cathedral in the old district, built in 1888 by a grief-stricken father who'd lost his daughter to influenza. Local legend said he'd incorporated his daughter's bones into the foundation stones, hoping to keep her close to him. They whispered about children's laughter echoing through empty corridors, about stained glass saints whose tortured eyes followed the living, about prayers that went unanswered but not unheard.

Perfect place for a meeting about the dead.

* * *

1 A.M. The iron church gates opened at Jason's touch with a rusty squeal that harmonized with the faraway police sirens in a symphony of urban decay. The sound followed him up the broken steps, past weathered stone gargoyles whose eyes seemed to track his movement with greedy interest. Each step felt heavier than the last, as if the very stone was trying to prevent his ascent — or perhaps urging him toward something inevitable.

Ahead of him the ancient cathedral rose against the sky like a wound in reality, its spires reaching toward heaven like accusatory fingers. Broken stained glass windows gaped like missing teeth, their remaining fragments catching moonlight in ways that made Jason's eyes water. The images they depicted seemed to shift when viewed indirectly — saints becoming sinners, angels becoming something else entirely, something that had never known grace.

The massive oak doors swung inward before he could reach for them, releasing the breath of centuries. Jason's eyes darted left then right, having trouble seeing anything in the gloom. Then he spied her, and his legs almost gave way.

Elena stood in the nave, beneath a towering wooden crucifix that cast its shadow across her like divine judgment. Moonlight through the fractured windows painted her in broken rainbows, but shadows clung to her black cloak like hungry children. Underneath her hat, Elena's hair had gone completely white — not the soft white of old age, but the stark, bleached white of bones left too long in the sun. One eye remained her natural sea-green, bright with borrowed pain. The other had turned midnight black, like a hole punched through reality itself.

"You shouldn't have come," she said, her voice echoing strangely in the vast space, each word returning distorted, as if the cathedral itself was mocking them. "But I knew you would. We always come when they call."

Jason opened his mouth to speak, but his windpipe tightened. Around them, the cathedral seemed to breathe with ancient lungs. The air hovered thick, tense, heavy with the scent of old incense and the burden of older prayers. Beneath it all lurked a sweetness like decaying flowers — the perfume of a freshly covered grave.

Jason gave her a befuddled look. Questions burned down into his belly, and drizzled through his brain. "Jesus, Elena, what —"

"Don't," she said, and cut him off with sudden sharpness. "Not here. Not His name. The dead don't like it. They remember too much about promises of resurrection."

Jason's stomach lurched. He could see the ink-blue moonlight reflected in Elena's eyes. She stood beside a stone baptismal font, its water black as oil in the darkness. As Jason watched, something rippled beneath its surface — though there was no wind in the cathedral to disturb it. The ripples formed patterns that stung his eyes to follow, like something trying to write messages in a language too old for human tongues.

"The dead are getting stronger," she said without preamble, her voice carrying the shock of dire prophecy. "Every time we open that door, they push harder to get through. And now..." She gestured to her darkened eye, where galaxies seemed to swirl in infinite darkness. "They're finding new ways in."

Jason began to feel woozy. He took a step toward her, but Elena thrust up a hand to stop him. The movement caused her skin to shift in the broken moonlight, becoming momentarily crystalline, the flesh glasslike and transparent. Beneath it, he could see hairline fractures running through her brittle bones, zig-zagging like a road map of loss, each crack glowing with an inner light that spoke of decay.

"You don't understand what we've awakened. What *I* awakened. First with Grace —"

"Grace?" Jason locked eyes with her, puzzled.

Elena's laugh was bitter as grave dirt. "My daughter. Did you think you were the only one? That grief like ours comes without a price? That the dead don't recognize the taste of parental pain?"

She moved to one of the broken windows, where moonlight bathed her in fragments of colored shadow, in bursts of liquid darkness. In the stained glass beside her, Jason caught a flickering reflection — a little girl in a flowing, sunflower-yellow dress, strawberry-blonde hair knotted in pigtails. *Is this her? Grace?* Jason's mind brimmed with throbbing anticipation. But when the girl turned around to face him, her eyes were black empty sockets, her smile jagged and grotesquely twisted, and her teeth stained red and growing darker by the second.

"Grace was six when the cancer took her," Elena continued, seemingly unaware of the reflection that rippled in the air behind her, and mimicked her movements in terrible parody. "I couldn't...I couldn't let her go. So I found ways to open doors that should stay closed." She touched the stained glass, and the reflection vanished like smoke. "But the dead don't come back the same. They come back hungry." Hearing that, Jason's heart stiffened, horrified; hadn't Kurt warned him of the same thing?

Elena didn't move. All at once the wooden conduit box appeared in her hands, though Jason hadn't seen her reach into her bag. She tightened her fingers around the curved corners. Its carvings writhed beneath her grip like living things trying to escape their prison. In the darkness around them, something that might have been moans and shrieks of pleasure echoed through the cathedral's bones, speaking in voices that sounded like children playing — if children's laughter could echo in reverse.

Jason could feel Elena's eyes watching him. "How long?" he asked, his voice sounding thin in the growing pressure. "How long have you been doing this?"

This brought a bitter twist to Elena's mouth. "Time moves differently when you walk with the dead." Her good eye fixed on him with terrible intensity. "The first door I opened was thirty years ago. Or yesterday. Or tomorrow. They don't experience time like we do. They experience..." She shuddered. "Hunger."

There she goes again with that word. The echoing laughter around Jason grew louder, and now it sounded like children playing games whose rules were written in blood. The shadows around Elena's feet began to move and slither and snake in ways that had nothing to do with the moonlight, forming shapes that suggested hands reaching up from beneath the cathedral's stone floor.

"They promised to let me speak to Grace again. And they kept that promise — technically. But it wasn't her voice I heard. It was never her voice." Elena's hands trembled on the box. "The dead lie, Jason. They wear the faces of those we've lost, speak with their voices, but they're not them. They're..."

She stopped as the cathedral's lone bell began to toll, though its tower had collapsed decades ago. Each bronze note felt like a hammer against Jason's skull, each ring carrying the weight of years of unanswered prayers.

"They're famished, and they're ravenous," Elena whispered, her voice barely audible above the impossible tolling. "And we've been feeding them. Every interview, every story, every moment of pain we broadcast — it makes them stronger. And now..." Her voice caught like fabric on old nails. "Now, Jason, they know about Judith."

Elena watched Jason's face with grim fascination. Judith's name hung in the air like unholy smoke from ritual censers, and the roar of children's shrieks and laughter around them grew teeth.

"What do you mean, they know about Judith?"

Elena's smile was terrible to behold — the smile of someone who had seen too much and understood too late. "The same thing happened with Grace. Once they knew how much I missed her, how much I blamed myself..." She looked up at the wooden crucifix. To Jason's shock, a rising heat seemed to puff around it. Tiny flames darted up the wood, and children's voices began to sing in shrill, ululating voices. "They offered to let me see her again. Really see her, not just hear her voice."

The toll of the phantom bell reached a crescendo, though now it sounded less like bronze and more like screaming. The stained-glass reflections on the floor began to shudder and writhe in ways that made Jason dizzy, whirling in patterns that suggested scenes from the life of a child — a child playing, a child laughing, a child dying.

"They'll offer you the same thing," Elena continued, her voice nearly drowned out by the shuddering wail of voices. "A chance to see Judith again. To hold her. To tell her you're sorry." She met his gaze with her mismatched eyes. "And when they do... you'll say yes. Just like I did."

Jason was suddenly frightened. He rubbed a hand over his mouth. "What happened when you said yes?"

Elena's face crumpled like ancient parchment. "I saw her. Held her. Told her everything I'd been holding inside." A single tear traced down her cheek from her darkened eye, leaving a burn mark on her skin. "And then I watched as something wearing her face told me exactly how she died. Every detail. Every agonized moment of pain. Every second I wasn't there to save her."

The phantom bell reached an impossible volume. The wooden crucifix shimmered and smoldered and crackled with fire, and the cathedral shadows began to coalesce into shapes that made reality shiver. Elena pressed the wooden box into Jason's hands. It felt warm to the touch, like something freshly killed, its heartbeat slowly fading.

"They don't want to help us find peace," she whispered. "They want to watch us suffer. Forever."

She turned to go, but Jason caught her arm. Her skin felt like ice beneath his fingers, and for a moment — just a moment — he saw what she really looked like to the dead. The sight would haunt his nightmares until the day he died, and perhaps beyond.

"Elena, wait! You said they offered to let you see Grace again. Was it...was it worth it?"

She looked back at him with eyes that had seen too much — one green as summer grass, one black as a starless sky. "Yes," she whispered. "That's why I'm warning you now. Because when they offer you Judith...you'll say yes too."

The bell cut off mid-toll, leaving a silence so profound it made Jason's ears bleed. Elena pulled free of his grip and hurried toward the cathedral doors. They opened for her like greedy mouths.

"One more thing," she said, pausing at the threshold to look back. "If you see Judith — if they show her to you — run. Run as fast and as far as you can. Because it won't be her." She stared from the doorway, and now both her eyes were midnight black. "It was never Grace either. I know that now."

Jason tried to cry out to her, to beg her to stop. But Elena stepped through the doors and vanished like she'd never been there at all. The silence that followed was alive with anticipation.

Now Jason stood alone. He tightened his fingers around the wooden conduit box, squeezing as hard as he had ever squeezed anything. As he did, the wooden box grew warmer, hotter. Then hotter. Its carvings pulsed beneath his fingers and thrummed like a heart. Or perhaps like something trying to get out.

Jason felt his mind groping for answers. For a moment he was wracked with a vast sense of helplessness, and wanted to follow Elena — but the idea sent a chill down his back. Then somewhere far-off in the cathedral's dusky shadows, he heard a child's laughter — high and sweet and terribly, terribly wrong. The kind of laughter that sounds like something trying very hard to remember how little girls are supposed to laugh.

Then another laugh joined it. This one he recognized. This one he'd heard every morning before school, every bedtime story, every moment of joy in a life cut too short.

"Daddy?" Judith's voice called from the darkness. "Daddy, I missed you."

The box in his hands grew hot as blood. Jason closed his eyes and began to cry.

And the shadows smiled with teeth made of memory and hunger.

The dead speak many languages.

But hunger speaks in only one.

And sometimes, in places where grief has worn holes in reality, that hunger wears the faces of those we loved most.

Those we failed to save.

Those we would damn ourselves to see just one more time.

CHAPTER TWELVE

The Weight of What Remains

Time folds like origami in grief's hands.

Three o'clock in the morning. Jason stood in Judith's old bedroom, Elena's strange wooden box burning against his palms…and remembered the sound of his marriage ending. Not the lawyers or the papers or the final slam of the door — but the silence that came before. The way he and Sarah had stopped speaking in full sentences, communicating instead in half-finished thoughts and averted eyes. The way they'd become ghosts in their own home, haunting different rooms, both trying to stay close to the empty space where Judith used to be.

The memory slammed Jason like a physical blow, a sledgehammer to his psyche: Sarah, three months after the funeral, folding one of Judith's sweaters with the careful precision of someone defusing a bomb. He'd found her that way so many times — holding their daughter's clothes, her toys, her school notebooks, as if these artifacts of interrupted childhood could somehow bridge the gap between living and memory.

After leaving St. Agnes, anxiety swelling in his chest like a balloon, Jason had driven from the cathedral into the suburbs, knocking and pounding on the door of the old family home until the new owners answered, then begging them to let him view his dead daughter's room, just one final time. He feared they might turn him away, thinking he was a madman, a lunatic, out of his mind, and he'd be reduced to a trembling puddle of tears on the porch. Yet they understood. They relented, ushering the grieving Jason inside.

Now he stood in the doorway of what had once been Judith's room. Moonlight spilled through the west window, turning the room into a museum of loss. In Jason's mind, everything was exactly as Judith had left it that final morning — her stuffed animals arranged by height, the tallest being Harold, her beloved and raggedy stuffed bear; her art supplies scattered across the desk, her last drawing still taped to the wall, waiting for colors that would never come. The air itself felt preserved, as if grief had become a preservative, keeping everything in perfect, terrible stasis.

"We need to talk about the room," he'd said three months later, catching Sarah once again smoothing nonexistent wrinkles from the fabric of Judith's favorite sweater.

Sarah's hands had stilled on the wool. "Not yet."

"It's been three months, Sarah."

"It'll be three months forever." She'd looked up then, her eyes fever-bright with tears or rage or both. "Is that what you want to hear, Jason? That I can't breathe in this house anymore? That every time I walk past her door, I forget she's gone, just for a second, and then I have to lose her all over again? That I've started counting my days in losses instead of hours?"

Jason bowed his head in remembrance. He'd reached for her, but she'd flinched away. That flinch became the period at the end of their marriage's sentence. A tiny movement that contained universes of pain, of failure, of things they couldn't say because saying them would make them real.

Now, standing in that same room, Jason's buzzing cellphone glowed with Sarah's name. The wooden box hummed against his skin, but for once, he wasn't thinking about the dead. He was thinking about the living — about how grief can become a third person in a marriage, demanding more attention than either partner has left to give.

The memory of their last marriage counseling session surfaced like a drowning person gasping for air. Sarah had broken down, sobbing and wailing, confessing that she'd been drinking heavily for months. This shocked Jason. How hadn't he known? The therapist then asked them to each describe their perfect day with Judith. Sarah couldn't speak, silent tears tracking down her face like rain on a window. Jason had gotten angry instead, shouting in a crazed rage that the question was callous, cruel, impossible. But really, he'd been afraid to answer because he couldn't remember anything except the last day — the screech of tires, the collision that ended the world, and the hellish echo of silence that followed.

"What are we doing?" Sarah had asked in the car afterward, her voice hollow as a church at midnight. "We're not healing. We're not even hurting together anymore. We're just...disappearing."

She'd been right. They'd become like binary stars after a supernova — locked in orbit around the same devastating absence, but spinning further and further apart until even gravity couldn't hold them together.

Out of the corner of his eye Jason stared down at his trembling hand. The phone kept buzzing. Sarah's name pulsed.

His hands shook as his fingertip hovered between the HANG UP and SEND TO VOICEMAIL buttons. Jason stared at both grimly. Finally he pressed the ANSWER CALL button, and spoke. "...Sarah?"

There was a pause. "Jason." Her voice was thick with sleep or tears or memory. "Do you know what time it is?"

He did. 3:47 A.M. The exact time Judith had been pronounced dead at St. Agnes Hospital. The time that had become their private midnight, the hour when grief kept its appointments with clockwork precision.

Jason cleared his throat nervously. "I've been thinking about the morning after," he said, the words coming before he could stop them. "When you made coffee and we both pretended we'd slept."

There was a sharp intake of breath. "Jason..."

"Let me finish. Please." He sank onto the floor, on his knees now, dust rising like years taking flight. "You were wearing her favorite sweater — the blue one with the rainbow. You'd pulled it from the laundry because it still smelled like her. And I couldn't... I couldn't look at you because all I could think was that I'd failed you both."

"Jason, don't —" Sarah pleaded.

"I was supposed to protect her," Jason's voice cracked like thin ice over deep water. "I was supposed to protect us. But I couldn't even protect you from me — from what I became after. The drinking, the anger, the guilt, the silence, the way I kept trying to disappear into work or sleep or anything that would make me stop remembering for five minutes."

The wooden box pulsed once, sharply, but he ignored it. This conversation belonged to the living.

"We both disappeared," Sarah said, and Jason could hear the unshed tears in her voice. "I'd sit in her room for hours, touching her things, and sometimes I'd look up and catch my reflection in her mirror, and I wouldn't recognize myself. Like grief had erased me and left this stranger wearing my face."

Tears rolled down Jason's cheek. He took a deep breath and then spoke. "I miss you," he said, the words falling like stones into still water. "Not just...not just then. Now. Still. Always."

Jason made no attempt to wipe away his tears, or to say anything else. The silence that followed felt different from their old silences. Less like a wall and more like a bridge waiting to be crossed.

"I started listening to your podcasts," Sarah said finally. "All those conversations with the dead...but..." she hesitated. "But you never tried to talk to *her*. Why?"

Jason hadn't expected the question. He bit his tongue to keep from answering. The wooden box grew warm against his leg where he'd set it, but its heat felt like a warning now rather than an invitation. Through the bedroom window, he could see the moon hanging low and full, painting the room in hazy shades of memory.

"Because I was afraid," he admitted. "Not of what she might say. Of what I might have to hear. About that day. About how I failed her. About..." he swallowed hard. "About how I failed us."

"Oh, Jason." Sarah's voice softened in a way he hadn't heard in years. "We failed each other. But maybe...maybe that's not the end of the story."

Not the end of the story? Jason pondered this. They were always a complete contrast in attitudes: Sarah starting conversations with strangers at the supermarket, with strangers on airplanes; Jason always the cool and aloof one, afraid of strangers. The memory gave him a helpless smile. Why hadn't their differences been a strength? He recalled the family photo on Judith's bedroom nightstand — that last perfect day at the beach. The sun caught them all in mid-laugh, unaware they were creating one of the final memories they'd share. But for the first time, he saw something else in the image: three people who loved each other completely, if imperfectly. Who might love each other that way again, if they were brave enough to try.

"Sarah," he said quietly. "I need to tell you something. About *Echoes*. About Elena. About... everything. And after I do, if you're willing... maybe we could try talking again. Not about who we were or what we lost, but about who we are now. Who we might still become."

On the other end of the phone there was silence. Vacantly Jason stared straight ahead, dazed and confused. *How could you have been so stupid?* he thought, anxious now about what he'd said. He felt lightheaded. The wooden box went silent, as if holding its breath. Outside, the city hummed with life and death and everything in between. And somewhere in the space between heartbeats, Jason sensed a seismic shift — not like an earthquake, more like a door slowly starting to close, or perhaps like one finally opening.

"I'd like that," Sarah answered gently. And in those three words, Jason heard something he hadn't dared hope for in years: the sound of chains breaking. The sound of grief transforming into something else. The sound of two people finding their way back from the dark, one trembling step at a time.

Scrolling desperately through the photos on his phone, Jason looked at Judith's picture one last time, at that captured moment of perfect happiness. "I'll always miss her," he said softly.

"I know," Sarah replied. "We'll miss her together."

And for the first time since that terrible morning, the weight of memory felt less like an anchor dragging him down and more like a compass pointing home.

Hours passed. The wooden box sat forgotten on the floor as Jason talked through the night with Sarah. Its carvings slowly stilled, its warmth fading like fever breaking. Whatever hungry things lived in its shadows would have to wait.

Some conversations belong only to the living.

Some wounds don't bleed. They echo.

Some healing happens only in the light.

And some loves, even broken ones, are strong enough to find their way back to wholeness — if only we're brave enough to take the first step, reach across the darkness, and say the words our hearts have been holding too long in silence.

After all, not all echoes are voices of the dead.

Some are the sound of life beginning again.

CHAPTER THIRTEEN

The Weight of All These Years

Memory has teeth that never dull.

Jason sat in his apartment, watching the podcast numbers climb on his laptop screen. Twenty million downloads. Thirty million. Each one a soul reaching into the dark, searching for answers in the voices of the dead. Each one feeding something that grew hungrier with every whispered confession, every shared secret, every moment of recorded grief.

He rocked backward in his chair, deep in thought. Eyes closed, he ground his forehead. The conversation with Sarah had kept him awake until dawn, their words etching new patterns over old scabs and scars. They'd talked about things they'd been too afraid to touch for years: the funny face Judith made whenever she was forced to eat vegetables, how she'd stick her tongue out when concentrating on her drawings, the sound of her feet running down the hallway every Christmas morning. Each memory a stitch in the tapestry of their shared loss.

"I used to pretend I was asleep," Sarah had confessed around 4 A.M., her voice soft and musical over the phone, gentle with remembrance, "when you'd sing that silly purple elephant song to her. But I listened every night. It was like a spell, keeping all three of us safe."

Until it wasn't.

Now, in the harsh fluorescent light of the kitchen, another conversation with the dead waited. Ernest Hemingway. The legendary American novelist, renowned for *A Farewell To Arms* and *The Sun Also Rises*, for his intense masculinity, and for his champagne-and-absinthe-soaked life that ended with alcoholism, depression, and suicide. The interview would break records, push *Echoes* into the stratosphere of podcasting success.

If he survived it.

Elena arrived exactly at noon, though arrived wasn't quite the right word. She seemed to fade into existence like a Polaroid photograph developing in reverse, each moment stealing more of her substance rather than revealing it. Touching the wooden conduit box Jason had placed on the kitchen table, it squirmed in her eerily-transparent hands, as if it was trying to sprout wings and fly away, flee its doom, escape its destiny.

Jason sat at the table, preparing his laptop for recording. Seeing Elena, he lost his balance, tipping backward in his chair. "Elena! What in the name of God —"

"Save your prayers," she sharply interrupted her voice sand-rough and ancient. "They don't reach where we're going."

A hollow feeling wriggled in the pit of Jason's stomach. Elena tried to keep her face hidden, the wide black brim of her hat scrunched low over her twisted brow. She looked worse than Jason had ever seen her. Her skin had gone beyond transparent — it was almost theoretical now, more memory than matter. Beneath it, her bones were traced with hairline fractures that seemed to be struggling to form words. Both eyes had gone midnight black. Tears leaked out from beneath her eyelids, each drop a different shade of sorrow.

"You spoke with Sarah," she hissed. Not a question. A statement heavy with knowing.

Jason was startled. "How did you —"

"I can smell the hope on you." Elena's star-filled eyes fixed on him with terrible intensity. "Like flowers blooming in a graveyard. Beautiful, but feeding on what's buried beneath." She snatched the carved box, placed it between them with infinite care, as if it might shatter at a touch. Or explode. "Hope is dangerous, Jason. It makes the living think they can outrun death."

Jason sighed, sat back in his chair. The recording light blinked red, ravenous as an eye. Elena drifted into her seat opposite him, and they began the next interview.

When Ernest Hemingway's voice emerged from Elena's bleeding lips, it carried the weight of all the world's winters. Edging forward in his chair, Jason leaned into the microphone.

"Mr. Hemingway, Ernest, I... it's an honor," Jason said, a shiver running down his spine. "Thank you for being here."

The famed writer they called "Papa" horse-laughed, his voice powerful and booming. "I'm just glad to be talking to someone who's interested in more than the surface of things. What do you want to know?"

"Ernest," Jason said, "your writing has had a profound impact on literature and on the way people see the world. But I know it came from a place of deep struggle, and anguish, of living through some of the darkest moments of the 20th century. Can you tell me what it was like for you to live with that intensity, to see and experience so much darkness?"

"Living... that's a funny word, isn't it?" Hemingway said. "You live through things, but they leave their mark on you. The war, the battles, the loves, the losses… they all took something from me, something I could never get back. But they also gave me something — a clarity, a way of seeing the world that was stripped of all the bullshit. You see, Jason, life is a battlefield, a war zone, and every day is a damn fight. You don't come out of it unscathed, but you do come out of it knowing what really matters. Courage, after all, is just grace under pressure…

"But you asked about the darkness," Hemingway continued. "The darkness comes in waves. First like a friend, offering rest. Then like a lover, promising peace. Finally like a child, begging to be held. That's the most dangerous darkness of all — the one that wears your children's faces."

Jason's hands tightened on his microphone. He hesitated. "Tell me about your children, Ernest," he said softly. "About what it means to leave them behind."

"My children?" Hemingway let out a sigh, as soft as cemetery grass. "I wrote each of my two sons a letter, you know. Tried to explain to them why I chose death. As if death could ever be explained to those left behind. But that's what we all do, isn't it? Try to justify our departures, our silences, our failures to stay."

"What did the letters say?"

"That the world is pitiless — it's callous, brutal, and hard. That sometimes love isn't enough to keep us breathing." Hemingway's gruff voice turned soft. "I lied, of course. Love was always enough. I just forgot how to feel it through the darkness."

Suddenly Jason heard a gasp. His eyes whirled to Elena. Elena's body convulsed, fresh blood tracking from her nose, her ears, her eyes. The wooden box pulsed with a light that hurt to look at, like staring into the sun's absence.

Feeling a hot blur of pain in his chest, Jason looked away, plunged ahead with the interview. "What would you tell them now, Ernest?" he hurriedly asked, thinking of Judith's last drawing still taped to her desk — their family portrait forever unfinished, waiting for the final lines that would never come.

"I would tell them..." Hemingway's voice softened. "I would tell them that every story I wrote was a love letter to them. That every word was trying desperately to build a bridge between my darkness and their light. That death lies, but love..." There was a pause. Jason took a deep breath, holding it in his lungs, and waited. "...But love tells the truth."

Elena's head snapped up, her eyes as red as comets, blazing with ferocious fire. "Stop!" she gasped, her own voice breaking through like shards of glass. "He's lying. They all lie. They show us what we want to see, tell us what we need to hear. But it's all just bait for their hooks."

"Elena —"

"Don't you understand?" Blood dripped from her lips like garnets. Her words exploded out, sounding scraped raw. "Every interview takes more! Not just from me — from *all* of us. We're feeding them our grief, our guilt, our desperate need to believe that death isn't the end. But it is! It always is!"

Convulsions thrashed Elena in her chair. Tears blinding her, she kept shouting. "They'll never let you go, Jason! Not while you still carry Judith's memory like a wound that won't heal! Not while —"

Another convulsion rocked Elena's body. Her knees quivered; more blood poured from her nose. Jason leaned across to take her trembling hand. As he did, the wooden box began to shake, its carvings writhing faster, forming patterns that made reality shiver. From somewhere deep inside it came a sound like children laughing. Or screaming. Or both.

Leaning away from her, Jason fumbled to turn off the recording. As if reading his mind, his phone buzzed. The name SARAH glowed on the screen like dawn breaking. Staring at the phone, a memory flashed through Jason's brain.

"I remember," Sarah had said last night, "the morning after...after it happened. You were making coffee like it was any other day. Like if we just went through the motions, maybe time would run backward. Maybe we could unmake what happened. But grief doesn't work that way, does it? It only moves forward, even when we're trying to stand still."

Jason's phone buzzed again. And again. Each time like a heartbeat refusing to be ignored.

"Choose!" Elena demanded, her body shuddering uncontrollably, her voice thick with blood and starlight. "The dead or the living. Memory or hope. You can't have both!"

Jason hesitated. The recording light still blinked, capturing it all. Twenty million listeners waiting for the next episode. Twenty million souls seeking answers in the dark.

But Sarah was waiting too. Sarah, who knew every layer of his grief, every shadow of his guilt! Sarah, who had loved Judith with the same fierce completeness, who carried the same weight of memory and loss.

Sarah, who was still breathing.

Jason reached for the phone. Pressed the ANSWER CALL button.

The second he did, the wooden conduit box exploded into fragments, showering them with splinters that burned like captured starlight where they struck. Elena wailed, put her hands over her face, painful, desperate wails and sobs shaking her. Into an exhausted heap she then collapsed, her body suddenly small and ancient and terribly, terribly human.

But Jason wasn't looking at her anymore. He was looking at his phone, at Sarah's text message:

I still remember all the words to that silly elephant song. Come home. It's time to start singing again.

Jason leaned back against his chair. The air shimmered between his shaky hand and the phone. And suddenly, he was crying.

He looked up at the apartment window. Outside, the sun broke through clouds that had lingered for what felt like centuries. Its light fell across the kitchen floor, across the recording equipment and his laptop, across Elena's crumpled form, across the shattered remains of the box that had contained so many hungry ghosts.

The dead speak in whispers.

But the living?

The living sing.

Bringing the phone to his lips, Jason took a deep breath. "Sarah," he whispered, wiping his eyes. "I'm ready to come home."

Arrows of sunlight pierced through the apartment window. Behind him, in the deepening shadows, Jason swore he heard the voice of Ernest Hemingway one last time: *"Love tells the truth."*

And for once, the dead weren't lying.

The dead were prophesying.

After all, some truths can only be heard when we stop listening to ghosts.

Some songs can only be sung by those brave enough to keep breathing.

And some love stories begin again only when we choose the living over the echoes of the dead.

CHAPTER FOURTEEN

The Space Between Heartbeats

Echoes fade, but love's voice remains.

The long drive to Sarah's apartment felt like crossing an ocean. Each mile stretched infinite with memory, with possibility, with fear. Jason's hands quivered on the steering wheel as morning fog rolled in from the bay, turning familiar streets and buildings into something dreamlike and strange. His phone lay silent on the passenger seat, though the shattered remains of Elena's wooden box had left splinters embedded in its screen like tiny accusations. Through the cracks, phantom voices from old interviews, old podcasts, played unbidden, each voice fighting to be heard:

"Fame is just another way of disappearing," Kurt Cobain's voice crackled through the static. "But love...love makes you real."

"The light's always waiting," van Gogh added from somewhere in the electronic depths.

"Sometimes goodbyes are not an ending," Marilyn Monroe murmured.

Jason's fists were sweating now on the wheel. The taste of ashes from the destroyed wooden box still lingered on his tongue. Elena's final warning echoed in his mind: *They'll never let you go. Not while you still carry her memory like a wound that won't heal.* The words made Jason's nerves sing like wires. In his mind he counted out the numbers. *Twenty million downloads. Twenty million souls reaching through the darkness, looking for answers.* But the only answer that mattered now was waiting in a garden apartment on the outskirts of the city, where life had learned to grow in broken places.

The voices of the dead faded as his GPS directed him to a small garden apartment complex near the college. The type of place people go to build a future, to start a life or start one over…or to hide. Maybe both. Potted plants lined the concrete walkway — not the carefully manicured kind, but survivors: hardy geraniums and stubborn succulents that thrived on minimal care. The kind of plants that refuse to die even when forgotten.

Sarah was waiting. Sarah, who had texted him the lyrics to that silly purple elephant song, complete with the hand motions they used to perform in perfect choreography with

Judith before bed. Each lyric a breadcrumb leading him home through the smothering fog of years and grief.

Sarah opened the door before he could knock. She looked both older and younger than he remembered — gray locks threading her dark hair like strands of summer moonlight, but her eyes clearer and brighter than they'd been in years. She wore one of Judith's old hair ribbons on her wrist like a bracelet, its faded colors a splash of childhood against adult skin.

"You look terrible," she smiled and said softly.

"You look alive," Jason replied.

Suddenly his phone sparked, Ernest Hemingway's voice emerging through the broken speaker: "The world breaks everyone, and afterward, many are strong at the broken places."

They stood in the doorway, the weight of all their shared years hanging between them like smoke. Finally, Sarah stepped back, letting him enter a space that felt more like a hushed and holy shrine to the memory of their lives together than an apartment.

The living room walls were covered with a collection of photographs — not just of Judith, but of all of them. Their wedding day. Family vacations. School plays. Summer softball games. The timeline of their happiness before it shattered. But mixed in with the old photos were newer ones: Sarah with a therapy group; Sarah receiving her 90-day AA sobriety chip; Sarah volunteering at a homeless shelter; Sarah planting a memorial garden at the children's hospital.

"You've been busy," Jason said, his throat tight with unspoken words.

"I had to be." Sarah touched one of the photos — Judith's last school picture, her buoyant little-girl smile missing two front teeth. "Otherwise the grief would have eaten me alive. Like it almost ate you."

Jason shivered. *Like it was still trying to eat me.* Even now, he could feel the pull of the dead, their hushed words promising one more interview, one more podcast, one more miraculous chance to hear voices from beyond. One more moment with Judith. If only Jason would put down the phone, and listen.

"The podcast...I..." he started, but Sarah cut him off. Her smile was sad but knowing.

"I've listened to all of them," she said. "Your interviews. Your ghosts. I needed to understand where you'd gone...I know about Elena. About Grace." She met his eyes steadily. "About what happens when we try to keep the dead from staying dead."

Jason sank onto her couch, suddenly exhausted by the weight of secrets. "How?"

"I've been watching you destroy yourself for two years, Jason. Did you think I wouldn't try to understand why?" She plopped down beside him, close enough to touch but not yet touching. "After I heard your interview with Vincent van Gogh, talking about how art comes from pain... I realized what you were doing with *Echoes*. You were trying to turn grief into something beautiful."

"I was trying to keep her close," Jason admitted.

"We both were. Just in different ways." Sarah looked at him and smiled. "I did research. Found others who'd worked with Elena. Or what's left of her."

Jason's eyes burned into Sarah's. "What do you mean?"

Sarah pulled out her phone, scrolled through it, and showed him screenshots of a curled and dog-eared photograph that made his heart stop. Elena, thirty years ago, standing in front of St. Agnes Hospital. She looked exactly as she had when Jason first met her — before the interviews had begun eating away at her substance. Jason was startled; he'd searched the internet without uncovering any trace of Elena. *How did Sarah find this?*

"I searched through the hospital records," Sarah confessed," and this is what I discovered. Grace died just before Christmas in 1989," she said quietly. "Elena started channeling the dead a week later. The first few times, it was just Grace. Then others started coming through. Each time taking a little more of Elena with them…

"The first was a father in 1990," Sarah said, showing him a yellowed article. "His son died in a car crash. Elena helped him make contact. A week later, they found him in his garage, the wooden box clutched to his chest. The article said he was smiling."

The phone crackled. Marilyn Monroe's voice, clear as a bell: "The dead know things, honey. We know when it's time to let the living live."

"There were others," Sarah continued. "A mother who lost twins to SIDS. A husband whose wife died of cancer. Each one thinking they were just doing interviews. Each one drawn deeper into the dark. But you were different, weren't you? You started asking them about life, not just death."

Jason shook his numb head. She was right. Somewhere between van Gogh's passion and Robin Williams' laughter, between Hemingway's courage and Plath's brutal honesty, the interviews had changed. Become less about grief and more about how to carry it.

Suddenly Jason felt Sarah touch his hand. "The more I researched Elena," she said, "the more I found. There are records — hospital visits, psychiatric evaluations. She should have died years ago, but something keeps her going. Something keeps feeding on her grief, using it to reach through to others who are drowning in loss."

"Like me," Jason said.

"Like us," Sarah corrected. "But I found another way." She gestured to the walls of family photos, to the life she'd built from the ashes of their shared tragedy. "We can't bring her back, Jason. But we can stop letting her death kill us, too."

As if in response, his phone buzzed. It was Elena's number, a text message. Jason rubbed his chin, stared at the phone in his palm, sighed and opened it. The message was simple:

One more interview, Jason. She's waiting.

Jason re-read the text, drew a long breath, losing control. Sarah saw the message. She took the phone from Jason's hand.

"She'll always be waiting. That's what the dead do. But the living..." She reached for his other hand, her touch electric with warmth, with possibility. "The living have to choose to live."

Jason looked at the photos on the wall — their history, their happiness, their loss. Then at Sarah, who had found a way to carry their daughter's memory without drowning in it. Who had built something new from the wreckage of their shared grief.

His phone buzzed again. Another text.

Please. She needs to tell you something.

Jason winced. He squeezed Sarah's hand. Tighter. Little by little, he regained control. And for the first time since Judith's death, the voices of the dead seemed fainter than the sound of Sarah's breathing beside him. Fainter than the rustle of wind through the memorial garden she'd planted. Fainter than the beating of his own, living heart.

"I don't know how," he admitted. "I don't know how to let her go."

"You don't have to let her go," Sarah said, clutching his hand. Dropping the phone, she brushed the hair from his sweating face. "Just let her rest. Let her be what she is —a beautiful memory, not a wound we keep reopening."

There was a moment of silence. Jason's eyes felt like they had sunken back into his head. Outside, the fog was beginning to lift, revealing a city painted in vivid colors of morning light. Somewhere in that light, Elena was waiting with her promises of one more conversation with the dead. One more chance to hear Judith's voice. One more. Always one more…

But Sarah was here, warm and real and choosing to live. Sarah, who knew every verse of that silly purple elephant song. Who carried the same burden of memory and loss, but had found a way to keep breathing beneath it.

His phone buzzed a third time. Then a fourth. A fifth. He didn't read the messages.

Instead, he looked at Sarah and asked the question he should have asked two years ago: "Will you help me learn how to live again?"

Her smile was like watching the sun rise after an endless night.

"That's why I'm still here," she whispered. And in her voice, he heard something he hadn't dared hope for in years:

A future.

The phone buzzed one final time, then went silent. Outside, the morning light grew stronger, the sunlight unseasonably strong, painting the world in colors the dead had forgotten how to see.

Some choices are made in darkness.

But the best ones — the ones that save us — are made in light.

And sometimes, if we're brave enough, they're made together.

After all, not every echo is a ghost.

Sometimes it's just the sound of love finding its way home.

CHAPTER FIFTEEN

What Light Remains

Heartbeats count time differently for the haunted.

St. Agnes rose against the dawn sky like a prayer carved in granite, each block laid by parents who had lost children to the influenza epidemic. Every stained glass window told stories of separation and reunion, of loss and redemption, of love that refused to die even when everything else had. The morning light struck the broken pieces now, painting the interior in fragments of meaning: blue for sorrow, red for love, gold for redemption.

Jason and Sarah found Elena inside, kneeling before the altar, beneath a massive stained-glass window depicting the resurrection. The glass was cracked but intact, showing a figure ascending toward light while mourners reached up from below with desperate hands. In the shifting dawn light, those hands seemed to move, eternally grasping for what they could not hold.

"I knew you'd come," Elena said without turning. "Both of you. The dead told me." Her voice echoed off stone walls that had heard too many desperate bargains.

Jason tried to answer, but the words were swallowed in regret. He felt Sarah leaning her head against his shoulder. Sarah's hand found Jason's, warm and alive and real. She wore Judith's rainbow ribbon around her wrist. The fabric caught the light from the fractured windows, throwing tiny rainbows that danced like the flame of memories.

"We needed to understand," Sarah said softly, her voice carrying in the vast space. "About Grace. About all of it."

Elena's laugh was dry as autumn leaves. "Understanding is what kills us in the end." She gestured to the empty air beside her, where a shimmer suggested the shape of a small girl. " Some cathedrals are built with stone. Others with grief. Grace has been waiting thirty years to tell me that."

Gazing around more closely, Jason's eyes widened. The cathedral seemed to breathe around them, decades of prayers and tears soaked into its bones. Through the broken windows, Jason could hear the city waking up — the distant morning murmur of automobiles and jet airliners, the hum of electricity buzzing through phone lines, the barking of dogs and the music of birdsong — all the mundane miracles of the living world. Each sound a reminder of what Elena had sacrificed, what he had almost lost chasing echoes in the dark.

"The interviews are over," he said, the words echoing off the stone walls. "It's time to let them the dead rest."

"Rest?" Elena turned finally, her star-filled eyes blazing. "The dead don't rest, Jason. They —"

"They *lie*," Sarah interrupted, but gently, like speaking to a frightened child. "Like you lied. About Grace. And about the others who came after Grace."

Elena went still as stone. Jason noticed the face in front of him change, as if her features were melting. In the silence that followed, the cathedral's ghosts seemed to lean closer, listening.

"Show them," Sarah continued, her voice steady. "Show them what thirty years of feeding on grief really looks like."

For a moment, nothing happened. Then Elena began to morph again, to undergo a shift. Not like before, not the theatrical transformation of channeling the dead. This was subtler, and much more terrible. The Elena standing before them now had been dead for a long time. Her eyes were glassy, like black marbles. Her face was bloated, like a corpse, her skin translucent, like looking through shards of cracked glass, then barely there at all. Beneath it, Jason noticed her bones were inscribed with the writing he'd seen before — now he saw thousands of names, dates, stories. All the grief she'd consumed over decades, written in a language of loss.

"Grace loved mornings," Elena whimpered, her form flickering between solid and spectral. "She used to wake me up by singing. Such a terrible voice really —but so full of joy. I'd forgotten that. I've been so hungry for her voice, I forgot the sound of her laughter."

Smiling, Elena fixed her black marble eyes on Jason. He stood frozen, unable to speak. Sarah stepped forward, still holding Jason's hand. "Judith was the same way. Remember?" she asked him. But Jason's focus remained fixed on Elena's eyes. Seeing this, Sarah pressed him. "How she'd wake us with that awful rendition of 'You Are My Sunshine'?"

A pain pierced Jason's heart, snapping him out of his reverie. "Until we taught her the purple elephant song instead," he said softly. "Because it made her laugh so hard she'd snort milk through her nose."

Sarah put an arm around Jason's shoulders. He drew himself upright, and they embraced in a tearful hug. Elena watched them, her galaxy eyes reflecting infinite grief — but now, something else too. Something like recognition. Something like dawn breaking after an endless night.

"Grace loved that song too," she sighed, and shook her head weakly. "I'd forgotten. I'd forgotten so much..."

A lump formed in Jason's throat. Reaching into his pocket, he removed the splintered and shredded pieces of the conduit box, placing them atop the church altar. The slivered remains lay scattered like fallen stars. Through the broken pieces, a single tiny voice emerged.

"It's okay, Daddy. Mommy. It's okay to let me rest now."

Judith! The voice drummed through Jason's skull. Seeing his pleading face, Sarah's hand tightened in Jason's. "That's not her," she said, trying to snap Jason out of his dream state. "The real Judith lives in our memories. In how she'd arrange her stuffed animals by height."

Jason stared down at his feet. "In the way she'd stick out her tongue when concentrating," he added, smiling.

"In her laugh," they said together.

Elena watched them with ancient eyes. "You're choosing the living," she said. Not a question.

"We're choosing each other," Sarah corrected. She reached into her bag and pulled out her phone, scrolling to the curled and dog-eared photograph — Elena and Grace at St. Agnes Hospital, thirty years ago. Both of them laughing, both of them alive. Both of them real. "And we're choosing to let you rest too."

Elena took the phone with trembling hands. As her fingertips touched the photo, gently stroking it, color seemed to seep back into her transparent skin. One of her midnight eyes cleared, becoming human again. She stared at the image like someone seeing sunlight after years in darkness.

"I made a deal," she said, as she handed the phone back to Sarah and eyed Jason. "After Grace died. Something lived in the spaces between grief and memory. It offered me a trade — I could speak to her, but only if I helped others do the same. Each interview taking a piece of me, feeding whatever lives in the shadows of loss." Her smile was terrible to behold. "I thought I was helping people. But I was just making them into fuel."

"But something changed," Sarah said softly. "With Jason. With *Echoes*. The interviews became different."

Elena nodded. "He started asking them about life, not just death. About love, not just loss. And they...they started answering differently." She looked at the photo again, tears tracking down her face. "They started telling the truth."

"Which is?" Jason asked.

"That love is the only voice that never dies." Elena's form flickered like a candle in wind. "The rest is just echoes."

Daylight all at once flooded into the cathedral. Shadows and reflections began to move, but differently now. Not like things trying to get in, but like things finally being set free. The air grew warmer, filled with the scent of Sarah's survival garden, of morning light, of life choosing to continue.

Elena's form became more solid with each passing moment, age and humanity returning to her features. The writing on her bones began to fade, names and dates dissolving like ice on the first day of a new Spring.

"Grace," she murmured to the shimmering spirit of a small child appearing beside her. "My beautiful girl. I'm sorry I kept you waiting so long."

A soft sigh escaped the shimmer. It took form one last time — a small girl in a sunflower yellow dress, whole and real and laughing. She reached for her mother's hand. Elena took it.

"Thank you," Elena said to Jason and Sarah. "For showing me what the dead have been trying to tell us all along — that grief doesn't have to be a prison cell. That love is stronger than death. That sometimes the only way forward is to let go."

She held tight to her daughter's hand. Together, they walked toward the altar, their glimmering spectral forms slowly dissolving, becoming transparent, then translucent, then barely there at all. The morning sunlight streamed through them, turning them to prisms that scattered rainbow fragments across the cathedral floor.

Then they were gone.

But something remained — not an echo, but a warmth. A sense of peace that filled the broken cathedral like sunrise filling a dark room.

Jason felt Sarah caress his arm. She leaned back against Jason, placing her head beneath his chin. Jason reached down and touched her cheek. Her hand was warm in Jason's, her heartbeat strong against his palm.

"What now?" Jason asked.

Sarah craned her head out from underneath his chin. She smiled — not the sad smile of shared grief, but something newer, something growing. "Now we learn to sing again."

The purple elephant song drifted through the cathedral one last time — not from ghostly voices or broken cellphones, but from two living people who had found their way back to each other. Their voices weren't perfect. They'd forgotten some of the words. But they remembered enough.

Sometimes that's all love needs to grow again.

Sometimes that's all life asks of us.

To remember enough, to sing anyway, to choose the light.

To let the dead rest while the living learn to dance.

Above them, the stained glass figures in the resurrection window seemed to shift in the strengthening dawn. But now the mourners weren't reaching up toward heaven.

They were reaching toward each other.

And the light pouring through the broken places was the color of healing.

The color of morning.

The color of love choosing to live.

CHAPTER SIXTEEN

Where Light Takes Root

Love grows in broken places.

The garden of survivors behind Sarah's apartment shouldn't have been possible. Concrete, lack of sun and overgrown weeds had choked the earth there, and ruled this space for decades. Now, impossibility bloomed. Sunlight flared down on the scarred soil. Rain fell gently, drenched the earth, and the wind scattered new seeds which took root. Lilies that glowed like moonlight, remembering Sylvia Plath's words about darkness giving birth to light. Sunflowers that tracked the sun like Vincent's endless quest for beauty. Wild roses that climbed in spirals like Kurt's defiant joy. Each plant a memory. Each memory a choice to live.

In the center, floating in a small pond that reflected the immense sky, was Judith's last drawing. They'd found it while finally cleaning out Sarah's storage unit together, the unfinished family portrait sealed now in glass. Their reflections completed the picture in the water — not the family they'd been, but the one they'd become. Whole in a way they'd never expected, broken in ways that let the light through.

"Sometimes," Sarah told the grieving parents and grandparents who came to her survival garden, "love grows better in broken soil."

She'd become known as the Memory Keeper among them. The one who showed them how to plant hope in winter. How to find beauty in broken places. How to keep breathing when breathing felt impossible. Her garden had become a sanctuary for those who carried losses too heavy to bear alone.

Jason watched her now from the kitchen window, the morning light catching Judith's ribbon on her wrist as Sarah knelt in soil that had no right to support life. But life grew anyway. Like love after loss. Like hope in darkness. Like them.

Like us, Jason realized.

His computer laptop sat open and humming on the table, displaying the final episode of Echoes. Not an interview this time. A truth:

"The dead speak in whispers," his recorded voice began. "But we the living sing. This is for everyone who's forgotten how. For everyone who's tried to talk to ghosts instead of each other. For everyone who needs to remember that grief isn't a purgatory, a prison cell or a grave — it's a garden waiting to grow."

The response had been beyond viral. Parents who'd lost children, children who'd lost parents, people broken by grief finding ways to bloom again. They came with plants and stories and hearts cracked open to light.

Like the young couple arriving now, carrying a small cherry tree and their son's favorite stuffed penguin.

"Tommy loved spring," Marie, the mother, said softly as Jason opened the door. "He'd count the buds on trees, make up stories about flower fairies. We thought... maybe..."

"Come," Sarah said, appearing with dirt-stained hands and clear eyes. "Show us where Tommy's stories want to grow."

They gathered in the garden, where morning frost surrendered to sun. Other memorial plants created a living tapestry: lily of the valley for Grace, brought by Elena's sister after hearing the podcast. Forget-me-nots for Kurt Cobain's daughter Frances. Marigolds for Marilyn's lost child. Each one a story choosing to continue.

As they dug the hole for Tommy's tree, more people arrived. They came every morning now, drawn by something stronger than grief. A father carrying his daughter's ballet shoes and a rosebush. A mother with her son's baseball mitt and a packet of wildflower seeds. A girl with her brother's Marvel comic books and a young oak sapling.

They formed a circle in the impossible garden, these pilgrims of loss transformed into gardeners of hope. Sarah showed them how to mix the soil with memory, how to plant love in winter, how to find life in letting go.

"The trick," she said, her hands gently grooming the earth, "is to give them room to grow, but make sure they're supported. And nourished. Like love. Like memory. Like us."

Jason knelt beside her, their fingers intertwining in soil that remembered how to bloom. Together they planted Tommy's tree, added his penguin to the growing memory wall, listened to his parents' stories until laughter mixed with tears.

"Will you sing it?" Marie asked softly. "The song from the podcast? About the purple elephant?"

Sarah caught Jason's eye, smiled. Not the sad smile of shared grief anymore, but something newer. Something growing.

Their voices rose together, not perfect but real. Others joined in, adding harmonies, creating something new from something broken. The garden seemed to listen, leaves turning toward their voices like plants seeking light.

Afterward, they sat in the memorial circle, drinking tea from mismatched cups donated by grieving families. Each cup a story. Each story a choice to live.

"I've been thinking about Elena," Sarah said quietly, touching Judith's ribbon. "About what she said at St. Agnes. About love being the only voice that never dies."

"She was right," Jason replied. "Just not in the way she thought."

A wind chime made from Grace's old toys caught the breeze, adding its voice to the garden's song. Somewhere, a child laughed — not an echo this time, but a real child, one of the many who came to play in this space where grief turned to growth.

The impossible survival garden bloomed on, each flower a memory made beautiful by choosing to live. Stories took root beside stories. Hope grew beside hope. Love learned new ways to speak.

Sometimes, in the quiet moments between heartbeats, Jason thought he heard familiar voices in the garden. Vincent van Gogh talking about the colors of the beautiful light. Robin

Williams speaking about the path to forgiveness. Kurt laughing about love's defiant joy. Not ghosts anymore, but seeds planted in fertile soil.

But mostly he heard the living. Sarah humming while she worked. Grieving parents sharing memories. Children playing tag between memorial trees. All of them choosing to grow through their broken places.

His phone buzzed — another message from his publisher, Jason's book chronicling the journey of Echoes already a roaring success. Jason smiled, remembering Elena's words about fame being another way to disappear. Pondering this, he plucked up the phone, and typed back:

Sorry. Too busy growing.

The garden needed tending. Stories needed telling. New purpose for his life needed excavating. Love needed room to bloom.

Sarah leaned against him, her heartbeat strong against his arm. Around them, the impossible garden stretched toward blue sky, each plant a testament to love stronger than death. Each flower a reminder that beauty grows in broken soil. And that the search for meaning in a constantly changing world ultimately leads one back home.

The dead speak in whispers.

But the living?

The living grow.

And sometimes, in gardens built from grief, in love that refuses to die, in voices choosing to sing together, something new is born. Something that blooms in the bitterest winter and grows through cracks and remembers how to live.

Not because they've forgotten.

But because they remember how to grow.

How to sing.

How to love again.

Jason watched as the young couple waved and climbed in their car and drove off. Sarah waved goodbye. Jason studied the shades of green in the garden, how Tommy's cherry tree caught the morning light, scattering rainbow fragments across the garden like promises. Like hope taking root. Like love beginning again. In the small pond at the center, Judith's unfinished portrait rippled with new reflections. New stories. New growth. New life choosing to continue.

Some wounds heal in spirals.

Some gardens grow through concrete.

Some love stories begin after the end.

And sometimes, in the space between heartbeats, in the silence between words, in the light between shadows, we find our way back to life.

Together.

Growing.

Remembering.

Living.

The survival garden bloomed on, defying winter, defying darkness, defying death itself. Each plant a story refusing to end. Each root reaching deeper into soil that remembered how to nurture life.

And in the gentle morning light, in this impossible flowering garden of memory and hope, something beautiful grew in the broken places, rising like a flame:

Love.

Taking root.

Blooming endless.

Beginning again.

EPILOGUE

Last night, I stood on the hospital roof again.

The parking lot lights still flickered through the fog like distant stars, but this time they looked less like surgical lights and more like beacons. The wind still sliced its precise cuts through my white coat, but now each gust carried something new: the scent of Sarah's memorial garden, the echo of healing voices, the sound of life choosing to carry on.

They don't teach you in medical school how healing works in reverse — how sometimes the doctor becomes the patient, the healer needs healing, the one who saves others must learn to save themselves. They don't tell you that some wounds are meant to heal imperfectly, leaving scars that map the geography of survival.

I think of my friend Peter now, not as an ending but as a beginning. His death cracked something open in me, in all of us who wear our white coats like armor and carry our stethoscopes like shields. Through those cracks, light found its way in.

Now when I make my rounds, I see medicine differently. Each patient's heart monitor tells two stories: the rhythmic beeping of their physical pulse, and the deeper rhythm of their human heart — the one that knows pain and joy, despair and hope, the endless systole and diastole of being alive. The thrumming drumbeat of life.

In the emergency room last week, a young resident pulled me aside. I recognized the look in her eyes — the same midnight despair I once saw in my mirror. "Sometimes," she confessed, "I feel like I'm drowning in other people's pain."

Closing my eyes, I thought of Peter. I took her to the roof. Not to the edge this time, but to the center, where you can see both the darkness and the dawn. "Look," I said, pointing to the garden below, where Sarah's memorial flowers bloom in impossible patterns. "Every crack is an opening for light."

The resident understood. Sometimes healing speaks in silence, in the space between heartbeats, in the pause between breaths. Sometimes the best medicine isn't in our prescription pads but in our presence — in showing others that survival is possible, that dawn always follows night, that being broken doesn't mean being destroyed.

I think of all the voices that helped me understand this: Vincent teaching me about beauty in chaos, Marilyn showing me how masks can become mirrors, Robin revealing how laughter can be both wound and bandage. Their ghosts have quieted now, replaced by living voices—Sarah's gentle wisdom, the stories of healing from the garden, the countless survivors who've found their way back to light.

In my office, I keep a collection of things patients have given me: origami cranes folded from prescription papers, sketches drawn during therapy sessions, letters from those who chose to stay. Each one a testament to the strength it takes to keep breathing when breathing feels impossible.

The medical texts call healing a process of restoration, of returning damaged tissue to its original state. But I've learned that some kinds of healing work differently. Sometimes we don't go back to what we were. Sometimes we grow into something new, something that defies logic, dedicated to the pursuit of a singular goal: to survive — like Sarah's flowers pushing through concrete, like love blooming in winter, like hope taking root in barren soil.

To those still standing on their own edges, looking down at their own indifferent stars:

Your pain is real. Your struggle matters. Your story isn't over.

Every crack in your armor is a place where light can enter. Every scar is evidence of survival. Every moment you choose to stay is an act of courage.

I'm no longer counting stars like pills or reasons to end it all. Now I count differently: heartbeats restored, lives renewed, moments of connection that remind us why we're here.

The world needs your voice. It needs your presence. It needs your particular way of being broken and healing and choosing to continue.

I'm still here to tell you this. I'm still here to show you how. I'm still here.

And I've learned that sometimes the most beautiful gardens grow in the most broken places. Sometimes the strongest healing comes from the deepest wounds. Sometimes the light we're seeking finds its way in through our cracks.

Hold on. Grow through. Bloom anyway.

The sun is always rising somewhere. And every dawn is proof that darkness is not the end of the story. It's just the beginning of how light finds its way home.

In the garden below me, Sarah is planting something new. Life continues. Love grows. And somewhere in the space between heartbeats, in the silence between words, in the light between shadows, we all find our way back to living.

Not because we've forgotten. But because we remember how to grow.

— Dr. Afshine Emrani

www.ingramcontent.com/pod-product-compliance
Lightning Source LLC
Chambersburg PA
CBHW060358310726
48976CB00003B/867